"A stronger, finer man would have sent you from his bedroom that night.

"Unfortunately, I was weak." Galen's voice dropped to a sultry whisper. "You make me weak. Even now."

Then he kissed her.

Despite his words, there was nothing weak about his kiss. Just as before, on that long ago night, his lips took hers with passionate possession, demanding that she surrender to his power.

How tempting he was! How dangerously, sinfully tempting…

But she had learned the consequences of giving in to such dangerous temptation. Verity broke the kiss and pushed him away. "Please, your Grace, go. I will explain tomorrow." That was another lie, yet she would sooner march into a den of starving lions than meet the Duke of Deighton alone.

His expression hardened. "I perceive that whatever attraction I held for you is quite finished."

"I was young and foolish then."

"I know, madam, so was I…!"

Dear Reader,

USA Today bestselling author Margaret Moore is known for both her Medievals and Regencies and we are very pleased to have her new Regency, *The Duke's Desire,* in the stores this month. This powerful tale is the story of reunited lovers who, for the sake of their secret daughter, must suppress the flames of remembered passion and outwit the blackmailer who is threatening to destroy them.

Dryden's Bride is a Medieval by Margo Maguire that features a lively noblewoman en route to a convent who takes a detour when she falls in love with a noble knight. For our Western readers, Liz Ireland's *Trouble in Paradise,* with a pregnant heroine and a bachelor hero, is waiting on the shelves for you. And in keeping with the season, don't miss *Halloween Knight,* complete with a bewitching heroine, a haunted castle and an inspired cat, by Maggie Award-winning author Tori Phillips. It's a delightful tale of rescue that culminates with a Halloween banquet full of surprises!

Whatever your taste in historicals, look for all four Harlequin Historicals at your nearby book outlet.

Sincerely,

Tracy Farrell
Senior Editor

MARGARET MOORE

THE DUKE'S DESIRE

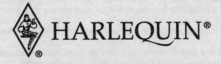

HARLEQUIN®

TORONTO • NEW YORK • LONDON
AMSTERDAM • PARIS • SYDNEY • HAMBURG
STOCKHOLM • ATHENS • TOKYO • MILAN • MADRID
PRAGUE • WARSAW • BUDAPEST • AUCKLAND

ISBN 0-373-29128-0

THE DUKE'S DESIRE

Copyright © 2000 by Margaret Wilkins

This edition published by arrangement with Harlequin Books S.A.

® and TM are trademarks of the publisher. Trademarks indicated with ® are registered in the United States Patent and Trademark Office, the Canadian Trade Marks Office and in other countries.

Visit us at www.eHarlequin.com

Printed in U.S.A.

Please address questions and book requests to:
Harlequin Reader Service
U.S.: 3010 Walden Ave., P.O. Box 1325, Buffalo, NY 14269
Canadian: P.O. Box 609, Fort Erie, Ont. L2A 5X3

To Melissa Endlich,
with thanks for putting out the fire.

Chapter One

Perched on the edge of a sofa in her ornately decorated drawing room, Lady Bodenham scrutinized the Duke of Deighton.

"Well, cousin," she observed with a maternal frown, "I must say the Italian air seems to agree with you, although you are quite brown."

She hit Galen's arm with her delicate ivory fan at each word. "Really…" Tap. "Quite…" Tap. "Brown."

Fortunately, her thin limbs seemed utterly without muscle, so her blows were no more disturbing to him than a piece of goose down.

Meanwhile, the Duke of Deighton's notoriously sensual lips curved up into a smile and his hazel eyes, twinkling with wry humor, calmly returned her perusal.

Eloise was as ornately decorated as the large room that had originally been part of a medieval abbey. Her family had gained possession of the abbey during the reign of Henry the Eighth and had been renovating it ever since, some with better taste than others.

Tonight Eloise wore a much trimmed muslin empire-waisted gown of pale green that regrettably brought out the green tinge to her somewhat sallow complexion. Her hair, which had never been fulsome, was tortured into a complicated style that made Galen want to wince as he speculated on the damage it must be doing to the scalp beneath.

"No doubt you spent far too much time living like a peasant," Eloise continued with a hint of petulance.

"Then I would have been a very wealthy and indolent peasant," he replied. "Tell me, is that all the change you notice?"

"Why, what else should I see? A tattoo or something equally outrageous?"

Galen didn't know why he had bothered to ask. Eloise had never been noted for her perception.

And as to his outward appearance, she was quite right. Save for tanned skin and a few wrinkles about the eyes, he didn't look much different than when he left England ten years ago.

He sighed as he turned his attention to Eloise's many guests, the usual collection of friends and sycophants who enjoyed his cousin's generous hospitality. Not unexpectedly, a few of them suddenly flushed and abruptly turned their attention elsewhere, away from him.

If only his reputation had died with his departure!

Unfortunately, it had not, something brought home to him the moment he entered Almack's upon his return. The unctuous smiles, the knowing smirks, the jests about locking away wives and sisters…

Ten years ago, he had been the most pompous, lascivious cad imaginable, a man who entered into and ended liaisons at a whim, or as if he were at the mercy of his lust and had no more morals than a dumb beast—until the night that had forever changed his life.

"I confess I cannot understand why you have lived abroad for the past ten years," Eloise declared.

Galen was extremely tempted to say it was because he preferred Italian peasants to his family and the British aristocracy in general, but he did not. After all, he was Eloise's guest, and no one was holding a gun to his head to force him to stay. "Because I like it."

Obviously offended by his cavalier response, Eloise said, "Perhaps you should have stayed there, then."

"I would have, if my father had not died."

Eloise reddened, and to lessen her embarrassment, he continued in the same casual tone. "So I have returned. However, dear cousin, you have not asked me why I have stayed."

"You have to run the estate," Eloise replied. "Or there is a woman, I suppose."

"No, I do not have to run the estate. Jasper can do that without my personal interference," Galen answered, naming the estate steward.

He moved closer to Eloise and dropped his voice to a conspiratorial whisper. "But you are right. There *is* a woman."

Eloise's eyes widened with avid curiosity as he hesitated melodramatically. "I have decided to find a bride."

Eloise stared in amazement. "A...a what?"

"A bride. A wife. A spouse with whom to share the remainder of my days, and incidentally provide an heir. I have come home to get married."

"I don't believe...I cannot comprehend..."

His brow furrowed with grave concern. "Shall I call a footman for a glass of water or smelling salts, Eloise? You seem on the verge of a fainting spell."

"No! No! I am not ill. I am shocked! Surprised! Delighted! Married! You!"

Although she ostensibly addressed him, her gaze eagerly searched the room.

"I have it!" she cried as if she had discovered El Dorado. With her fan she surreptitiously gestured toward a young woman in a gown of virginal white with a pink sash and pink tea roses in her glossy black hair. Her complexion was pink and white, too, and she had a long, graceful neck adorned with a relatively plain, thin gold chain.

Eloise's voice dropped to an excited whisper. "Lady Mary, the Earl of Pillsborough's daughter! Her fortune is *immense*. You could do much worse, Galen, much, much worse, for as you see, she is a beauty, too."

A beauty, perhaps, he inwardly agreed, yet he had seen many beauties, and it would take more than physical appeal to persuade him to marry.

"She's very accomplished, too. She plays and sings and nets the most exquisite reticules—"

He interrupted Eloise before she had him engaged. "I was not planning on making a selection today."

Eloise frowned. "It's not as if you are young, you know, Galen. You're over thirty."

"I know I have wasted quite enough time, Eloise, but I had my reasons."

"Oh?"

"Private and personal reasons, cousin."

Eloise's frown deepened. "Oh."

"I do stand in serious need of your superior knowledge of the ton, however," Galen said, not only because he did, but to placate her wounded feelings. "I wouldn't want to be carried away by a pretty face or charming manner."

Appeased, Eloise smiled. "I shall be delighted to be of assistance, Galen, delighted!" Then she frowned again.

"What is it? Is there someone unsuitable here possessing a pretty face and charming manner? How pretty and how charming, and in what way unsuitable?"

"As a matter of fact, yes—not for the reasons you might think, or reasons you might hear from other people."

"My dear cousin, you have me all agog with curiosity," Galen replied, only slightly exaggerating.

"She's a very dear friend of mine from my school days."

Galen could remember the younger Eloise. What a giggly creature she had been, and if her "very dear friend" was similar, Eloise's warning was quite unnecessary.

"She's a widow. Her husband passed away two years ago and she's been practically a *hermit* since it happened."

Galen made a wry smile. "It was my understanding, cousin, that hermits are all men."

Her fan fluttering about as if she were fending off an attack of moths, Eloise gave him a sour look. "Recluse, then. Whatever you wish to call it, it's taken this long for her to come for a visit."

"I don't see any women wearing black," he observed after a quick scan of the bevy of silk-and-satin-clad ladies.

"She isn't here yet," Eloise replied. "She should be down shortly, unless her daughter has made some sort of fuss. She simply dotes on the child and will spoil her completely if she's not careful."

Galen's smile tightened imperceptibly. "I trust you have given her the benefit of your advice," he remarked. Eloise's opinions were very decided for a woman who had never been a mother.

"Naturally, but I doubt she will pay any heed. She was always stubborn."

"Then relax anew, cousin. I make it a policy to avoid stubborn women, and stubborn widows with children fill me with horror."

"Please don't talk like that around my friend! You'll scandalize her, I'm sure."

"We wouldn't want any of your guests scandalized," Galen agreed, thinking how much it would take to truly scandalize most of them. "So, once we are introduced, I will ignore her," he said.

His slight sarcasm was utterly lost on Eloise. "I know I can't expect that. Everybody knows you can't leave a pretty woman alone. Just don't flirt with her, or I'm sure that will send her scurrying back to Jefford as quick as a wink. She *has* heard about you, you know. Indeed, I fear...'' Eloise flushed. ''Well, I may have painted a rather... vivid...portrait of you.''

Galen could easily imagine how Eloise had described him and his activities before he left England. The widow would likely expect him to have horns and a tail.

''Mind you, she isn't as pretty as she used to be.''

''Her husband's death had a serious effect on her looks?''

''She was quite undone by it. Frankly, I thought he was rather old for her. Still, he adored her, people say, and was delirious with joy when they had a child, even if it was not a son.''

Eloise shifted closer, unfortunately bringing the heavy scent of her perfume with her. ''Her in-laws were furious, I understand. For years they were quite certain they were going to get the old man's money, you see, and then not only does he marry, but along comes a child. The principal of his estate went to her. Her mother has an allowance from the interest. The in-laws only got a small bequest. Indeed, I heard tell they were quite nasty when Daniel Davis-Jones died, and even suggested an *inquest*.''

''Was his death so mysterious?''

''Well...'' Eloise leaned even closer. ''It was

rather sudden. Nevertheless, the doctor was absolutely sure it was pneumonia. How anybody could *think* his wife could be capable of…'' She raised her brows suggestively.

''Murder?''

''Don't say that!'' Eloise cried, truly horrified. ''You won't consider it, either, after you meet her. She's the most gentle creature!''

''You are the one putting such thoughts in my head,'' Galen observed. ''However do you learn these things?''

''I have my ways, Galen.''

Of course she did. She gave parties, had houseguests nearly continuously, took the waters at Bath and Baden-Baden and wrote letters. She had a network of gossiping friends that would likely put the government to shame when it came to gathering information.

''Oh, dear, I think I've made a serious mistake,'' Eloise said with as much remorse as he had ever heard her express. ''You sound fascinated.''

''Ancient gossip really doesn't interest me, and I assure you, cousin, that widows with children and no large estate hold absolutely no allure.''

''Good. Now come along and let me introduce you to Lady Mary,'' Eloise said, nodding at the young lady across the room.

''I think I need a moment to compose myself before this important introduction,'' he answered, telling a partial truth. "If you'll excuse me, I believe a brief turn around your lovely gardens will be just the thing."

Before Eloise could protest, Galen turned and strode out onto the terrace. A swift glance over his shoulder told him Eloise had not followed, and he sighed with relief.

He did welcome the fresh air, away from the scent of perfume and pomander and wig powder, for some of Eloise's older guests still favored wigs.

He should have known better than to take Eloise up on her invitation to stay at Potterton Abbey anytime he found it convenient. He had forgotten that she would consider her house empty if she had anything less than twenty guests.

And now that he had told his voluble cousin his plan, he felt as if he might as well have set himself up for auction. Somebody should hang a placard around his neck reading, "For Sale, One Duke, in slightly used condition."

He paused a moment and slowly surveyed Eloise's garden. She was a gossiping, usually harmless busybody, but she did have beautiful gardens. He inhaled deeply, encountering some scents that were universal, like the damp greenery, and others— ephemeral and unnameable—that told him he was in England.

Was there any green anywhere that could compare with the English countryside?

With another sigh, he headed toward the shrubbery. In theory, the bushes were supposed to represent untrammeled nature. Eloise, however, would no more allow nature to run wild within her domain than she would allow her husband to get a word in edgewise during a game of whist.

Still, a shrubbery was a shrubbery, which meant he could count on some privacy. If he was avoiding company in a way that could almost be termed hiding, he really didn't care.

"Sir!"

Alerted by the warning cry, Galen ducked as some kind of missile flew past his head. "What in—!"

"I'm sorry!" a little girl called as she ran toward him from the shrubbery. She picked up her ball and paused awkwardly, blushing and regarding him with brilliantly blue eyes beneath a riot of dark curls. "I didn't know anybody was nearby when I kicked it," she continued in soft and sorry tones.

She could have been any age from eight, if she were tall for her age, to twelve, if she were short. She was well dressed in a dark garment devoid of ornamentation, which bespoke mourning, and made of fine enough fabric that he guessed she was the child of one of Eloise's many guests.

His heart went out to a child who had cause to wear mourning clothes, especially this sprite of a girl whose bright eyes made him think she really ought to be wearing something pastel and decorated with flowers.

Then he wondered if this was the daughter of Eloise's bereaved friend, the stubborn widow who had lost her looks.

If that was so, Eloise was wrong in her estimation that the girl was spoiled. He had very intimate knowledge of spoiled brats, and this child didn't fit the mold. His youngest half brother would have chastised him for getting in the way without a moment's hesitation.

"That's quite all right," he assured her, giving her a smile. Galen Bromney's smiles were not particularly rare; however, a sincere smile on his face was. "I'm glad to know I was not under attack."

The girl's eyes widened as she clutched her ball close. "Have you ever been under attack?"

"Once or twice," Galen replied ruefully.

The girl's mouth formed an awestruck circle.

"At the risk to my reputation, and to be completely honest," Galen confessed, "the weapon was words, not a sword."

The child's face fell and quite suddenly Galen felt the most outrageous sense of loss. "Allow me to introduce myself. I am the Duke of Deighton," he said formally, making his very best bow.

He was absurdly pleased to see the awe return to her blue eyes as she made a graceful little curtsy.

"I am Miss Jocelyn Davis-Jones," she replied gravely.

"How do you do, Miss Davis-Jones?"

"Very well, thank you, Your Grace."

He was impressed that she knew the proper form of address. "Are you all by yourself?" he asked, looking around for other children.

"Yes," she said in a tone that was both hurt and defiant.

She must have seen the puzzlement in his face. "They didn't want to come outside, so I came by myself. I don't mind being alone."

"Admirable independence, Miss Davis-Jones."

"I would rather be at home. I don't like it here."

"I am sorry to hear that."

The child flushed. "Lady Bodenham is very nice, and her house is wonderful, and her cook makes lovely puddings, but I miss my own house."

"I do, too," Galen confessed. "My house is in Italy."

Her brows furrowed. "Are you Italian?"

He shook his head. "No, but I have lived in Italy for the past ten years, and I think of it as my home."

Indeed, his villa was more of a home than his family's seat had ever been, even if it could be just as lonely.

"Oh. I suppose I had better go in for tea now."

"I don't think it's quite time yet," Galen said. He nodded at the ball in her hands. "I haven't played football for a very long time. Would you like to play a game?"

Jocelyn Davis-Jones tilted her head and scrutinized him skeptically. As she did, he realized he wanted this child to like him, although he couldn't say why.

"You might get your clothes messy."

Galen suspected this warning had been given to her many times. "I am willing to accept the consequences," he declared bravely.

He was rewarded with a smile before the girl put the ball on the ground. While Galen wondered if her bountiful curls were natural, she suddenly— and without a word of warning—kicked the ball directly at him.

With a dexterous leap, he eluded it, then scrambled to catch the ball with his foot. He kicked it back toward Jocelyn while he crouched down in anticipation of the next kick, regardless of the crease of his trousers or what his valet might say.

The little girl was fast, and soon had the ball between her feet. In another instant, it came flying along the ground toward Galen, who threw out his leg in a wild and foolish attempt to stop it.

With a roar of dismay and not a little pain, he fell to the ground.

"Are you hurt?" Jocelyn cried worriedly.

"No," Galen muttered as he grabbed the ball and got back on his feet as fast as his thirty-year-old legs and one slightly pulled muscle would let him.

He held the ball out, dropped it and caught it midair with a kick. With a bleat like a lamb, she was after it and Galen took a moment to brush bits of greenery from his trousers.

At the sound of a foot colliding with the ball, he looked up, then dashed across the open space to intercept. He gave a cry of triumph as he returned the ball without having to bring the rolling object to a complete stop.

The child ran the other way to catch it, but before she could, it disappeared under a particularly bushy shrub. Bending over, she peered under it. "I can't see where it went!"

Galen hurried to help her look for it.

They were both bent over and scanning the thick trunks and branches of the smoothly pruned bushes when they heard a woman calling Jocelyn's name.

His companion straightened. "That's my mama. It must be time for tea." She glanced worriedly at the bushes that had apparently swallowed up her toy. "She'll be upset if I've lost my ball."

"Then I shall stay and look for it," Galen offered. "I'm sure it can't be far—although I did give it a prodigious kick."

"It was a crocked kick, or I would have caught it," Jocelyn declared.

"It went exactly where I meant it to go. Or rather, in the right direction," Galen replied defensively.

Jocelyn's expression betrayed her dubiousness. "You wanted it to disappear in the bushes?"

"No, of course not. I was aiming for you."

"But I was way over there!"

"Well…" Galen had to laugh. "Very well, my aim was off—but you were moving in this direction, weren't you?"

"Jocelyn?"

Galen and his little friend both turned to find a young woman looking at them quizzically.

Verity Escombe.

At the sight of her instantly recognized face, a host of emotions shot through Galen—of joy, dismay, anger and excitement.

He took a step forward, then caught himself.

He had never wanted to see her again. During these past ten years, he had hoped he would never see her again. Good God, why did he have to see her again?

It had been ten years, yet Verity Escombe was much the same, with those questioning blue eyes that her daughter had inherited and her lips parted as if about to ask a question, or in anticipation of his kiss.

He noted her gown of plain black, with a high waist in the fashion of the day. A thin black lace shawl covered her slender shoulders. Her light brown hair was simply and plainly dressed, and she wore no gloves.

He looked at her left hand and saw the wedding ring.

"Mama, this is the Duke of Deighton," Jocelyn announced, hurrying forward and taking her mother by the hand to lead her toward him. "We've been playing."

He glanced at the child. No matter how he felt about Verity, he wouldn't hurt her little girl by being rude, so he bowed elegantly and spoke as if he had never met Verity Escombe before.

As if, ten years ago, she had not seduced and abandoned him.

Chapter Two

Completely shocked, her heart pounding, an excitement she couldn't subdue battling with dread, Verity's mind raced back to the last time she had seen the Duke of Deighton.

Naked, he had sat up in his bed and begged her to tell him what was the matter. Sobbing with remorse for her selfish, lascivious act, she had not answered. She had run away as fast as her trembling legs and bare feet could take her.

Afterward, desperately hoping she would never see Galen Bromney again, she had hurriedly departed the house where they had both been guests, giving Lord Langley the excuse that she was needed at home.

Now here he was, looking as handsome and elegant as when she had first set eyes on him ten years ago. His eyes shone with that same mixture of apparent interest and self-confidence, and his smile still seemed to offer a great compliment.

And even after all this time, he continued to wear his dark, waving hair rather unfashionably long.

Before she had met him, she had heard speculation that the notorious Duke of Deighton thought himself some kind of Samson to have such hair, although few men could boast shoulder-length curling locks and yet look so undeniably masculine. Indeed, his hair gave him a hint of the savage, implying that he was capable of primitive passion.

So she had felt the first time she had laid eyes on him, and so, she realized as heat blossomed within her, did she still.

As for the duke's sexual prowess, she knew for a fact it was not exaggerated.

She looked at her daughter, who was ignorant of any relationship between her mother and this man.

Jocelyn must remain ignorant, and so must everyone else, unless their lives were to be fodder for gossip and scandal, and her daughter face a future of undeserved notoriety.

"I am delighted to meet you," the duke said in that smooth, deep and seductive voice no other man possessed.

"You must be Mrs. Davis-Jones, if this is your daughter," he remarked with another little bow.

"Yes, I am, Your Grace. Come, Jocelyn, we must excuse ourselves and go in for tea," Verity said, without meeting his gaze.

"Are you coming in for tea, too?" Jocelyn asked him.

"No."

Verity began to breathe again.

"I intend to take another turn about the garden before I enter the lion's den," he added.

"There are lions here?" Jocelyn demanded excitedly, obviously expecting to find a menagerie somewhere on the grounds of Eloise's estate.

The duke chuckled softly, and Verity noticed the wrinkles around his eyes. "A figure of speech only, I'm afraid."

Verity took a firm grip on her daughter's hand. "Come along, Jocelyn. We mustn't be late for tea."

She felt Jocelyn's reluctance, yet she ignored it. "We mustn't keep the others waiting, and I'm sure the duke has...wishes..."

He smiled as her words trailed off. "She has been very pleasant company."

"There's my ball!" Jocelyn suddenly cried, pulling away from Verity to retrieve her toy from beneath a bush a few feet away.

Leaving Verity almost alone with the Duke of Deighton—a smiling, seductive, still oh, so desirable Duke of Deighton.

She rushed after her daughter and again took her by the hand.

"Goodbye, Your Grace," she said as she led Jocelyn away with all the dignity she could muster, which was quite considerable.

"That is more than you said the last time, my sweet," the Duke of Deighton murmured as he watched them disappear from sight.

"I don't understand it. We just arrived," Nancy Knickernell muttered emphatically as she obeyed her mistress's request to pack their bags.

Seated at the lovely mahogany vanity table where she was putting the finishing touches to her hair before going below to join Eloise, Lord Bodenham and the other guests before dinner, Verity could see Nancy—and her frustrated expression—in the vanity mirror.

Nancy's tone, however, was always emphatic and her expression often seemingly annoyed, so much so that when Verity had first come to live with Daniel Davis-Jones, she had feared Nancy didn't like her. It was only after several days that she realized a sort of disgusted, emphatic tone was Nancy's typical one.

"It *is* lovely here, and it was kind of Lady Bodenham to invite us, but I think we have stayed long enough," Verity replied. "Jocelyn is anxious to get home, and so am I. Besides, Lady Bodenham has more guests arriving every day now, and I would rather be at home than in a great deal of company. I was not as ready to be among strangers as I thought.''

The much-freckled, red-haired Nancy straightened and hurried to take the young widow's hand. She patted it sympathetically. "Don't pay no mind to me. I spoke without thinking.''

"No, I'm sorry to be such a bother,'' Verity replied. She was also sorry to have to lie to the woman who was more like a kind and helpful older sister than a servant, yet she had no choice.

Just as she had no choice except to get Jocelyn away from this place and safely home again.

Despite that fervent desire, she dared not keep to her room tonight, tempting though it may be. To do so might make people think about her more than they would otherwise, and cause unwelcome speculation.

"How do I look?'' she asked as she stood and slowly turned in a circle for Nancy's critical scrutiny, pretending she was well content with her clothing and hair.

In truth, she wished she did not have to wear black anymore, and that she dared to dress her hair with more style.

"Pretty as a picture, and no mistake,'' Nancy said.

"Well, maybe it's better we're getting away

from these nobs and their servants," she continued with a philosophical sigh. "My word, some of them is as arrogant as their masters and no mistake. This valet come today—he's the pip, he is. Tried to tell me his name was Claudius Caesar Rhodes.

"'If that's true, then I'm Queen of Sheba Knickernell,' I told him."

Verity smiled and pitied the poor, unsuspecting fellow, for she could well imagine the venom Nancy had infused into that remark.

"He's the Duke of Deighton's manservant, though, so what could you expect?" Nancy eyed her mistress shrewdly. "Is that why you want to go?"

Verity struggled to betray nothing. "Why would I leave just because the Duke of Deighton has arrived?"

"Because you're a beautiful woman, that's why. Everybody's heard about the duke and women. I heard tell he's had so many lovers, when somebody asked him to name them all, he couldn't do it."

"Or wouldn't, perhaps, if someone was so impertinent as to ask such a question. Besides, he would have no interest in a widow of my age."

"Lucky for you!" Nancy's expression changed to one of avid curiosity. "It's true that he's had lots of lovers, isn't it? Some Parisian actress, and one that he more or less gave to the Prince Regent?''

"Nancy!"

"Well, you've known Lady Bodenham a long time, and she's his cousin, so she might—''

Nancy fell silent when she saw her mistress's look. "I was just thinking aloud," she muttered as she went back to the packing. "Excuse me, I'm sure."

Verity sighed softly. She couldn't fault Nancy for her speculative remarks, for in truth, Eloise had often regaled her equally curious friends with tales of her cousin's supposed liaisons and bets and duels.

If she hadn't, Verity thought bitterly, perhaps *she* might not have been so fascinated by him, and so excited when she first met him.

"Your hands are shaking," Nancy noted, her tone at once wary and accusing. "Are you sick? Is that why you want to go home?"

"No, I'm not ill, only tired," Verity answered. "It's difficult staying up so late. I'm not used to the nobility's hours."

"Or that Lady Bodenham's tongue wagging everlastingly, I don't doubt," Nancy said as she started to fold one of Verity's plain petticoats. "She only asked you here because she was curious to see you in widow's weeds, if you ask me."

"Nancy!"

"Well, it's true," Nancy answered defiantly.

"Partly, perhaps," Verity agreed. "So it's not so very strange that I want to go home, is it?"

"Not a bit, and 'scuse me for kicking up any fuss at all. When are we leaving?"

"I shall ask Eloise if we may have a carriage to take us to the inn for the post chaise early in the morning. You will be able to have everything packed in time, won't you?"

"Oh, aye, I will," Nancy confirmed.

"Thank you. I shan't stay late below."

After Nancy nodded, Verity went into the adjoining bedroom. It was really intended to be a dressing room, but rather than have Jocelyn far away in the nursery, Verity had asked Eloise to fit it up as a bedchamber. Nancy also slept here, so between their cots, there was not much extra room.

Jocelyn was already washed and in bed. A single candle burned on the small table beside her.

"You look pretty, Mama," Jocelyn said with a satisfied smile.

"Thank you." Verity tucked the covers around Jocelyn's shoulders. "Try to go right to sleep, little girl. We shall have to be up very early in the morning."

"I don't want to go home."

Taken aback, Verity sat on the bed. "I thought you didn't like it here."

"That was before I met the duke."

Verity briskly tucked the covers around her some more. "Won't you be happy to be back home?"

"I liked him. He was jolly. Not what I thought a duke would be like at all. He's not very good at football, but he tried. Didn't you like him?"

"He seems nice."

"I thought we weren't leaving till Friday. That's another four whole days."

"I know, dear. However, Lady Bodenham has so many other guests now, and I am feeling a little homesick, so I thought we should leave.

"Now be a good girl and try to get to sleep. We have a long journey ahead of us—but home will be at the end."

Still not mollified, Jocelyn nevertheless nodded and snuggled beneath the covers. "I wish I could say goodbye to the duke."

"Nancy's got to finish the packing. She'll be in the other room if you need her," Verity said, ignoring her daughter's comment. She blew out the candle. The moonlight bathed the small room in silvery light. "Good night, sleep tight, my little girl."

"Good night, Mama."

Outside in the corridor, Verity took a deep breath before heading below to Eloise's finely furnished drawing room. There were several other guests already in attendance, including, she noted at once, the Duke of Deighton, leaning against the mantelpiece and smiling at young Lady Mary.

She wouldn't look at him again if she could avoid it, Verity vowed as she continued to scan the room for Eloise. Not when he looked so handsome and elegant in his black evening dress, his pose casual yet reminiscent of a lion sleeping in the sun.

A lion quite capable of pouncing and trapping his prey, if he so desired.

Unfortunately, Eloise was nowhere to be seen. Perhaps she was still upstairs trying to coax her husband into his evening dress. It was no secret that Lord Bodenham detested parties of any sort, unless they were hunting parties involving horses and his beloved hounds.

Well, she could not linger at the entrance like a dressmaker's dummy, Verity thought, so she started toward the group of women nearest to the door.

"There was that actress at the Royal Theater, and then the dancer from Paris," the wife of General Ponsonby said excitedly as Verity came near the small cluster of women wearing very lovely, expensive and colorful gowns. They were also laden with jewelry, and their ornate hairstyles were adorned with pearls, feathers and ribbons.

Verity told herself she should not feel like a pauper at the feast. She had every right to be here, and she was, after all, in mourning.

Nor did she wish to attract any attention to herself, in any way, from anyone.

"And the Duchess of—"

The thin, middle-aged woman fell silent when she saw Verity, then ran a measuring and slightly scornful gaze over her.

Verity instinctively clenched her teeth, wondering if the woman was condemning her for her lack of fashionable style or recalling past scandals. "Pray do not let me interrupt you," she said as graciously as she could.

The general's wife glanced toward the duke. "It is not important."

"I assume you were speaking of the Duke of Deighton," Verity proposed.

She moved conspiratorially closer to Lady Smurston, a large woman wearing an ill-fitting gown of purple that strained against her ample bosom. The gathers at the high bodice did nothing to disguise her equally ample stomach.

"I confess he quite frightens me," Verity continued. "He looks so fierce, if he speaks to me, I should probably swoon."

"I daresay *you* will be quite safe," Lady Smurston replied. "He's looking at Lady Mary now, and she seems pleased to be the object of his scrutiny. I imagine she's already planning her wedding clothes."

"Oh, surely she knows better!" the gray-haired,

black-eyed Lady Percy cried. "Those bad Bromney boys won't settle down till they're fifty, if then!"

"I didn't know the duke had any brothers," one of the other ladies remarked.

"Oh, indeed, he has," Lady Percy answered eagerly. "The late duke had two wives, you see. Deighton is from his first—to the Earl of Hedgeford's daughter. After she died, the duke married Lady Crathorn, a great beauty—and proud of it, too. Marrying the duke made her quite insufferable, really. The names she chose for her children! I'm sure she was determined to remind people of her family's history. Each one is the title of a family into which the Crathorn women have married, at one time or another."

Another younger woman, so pale Verity thought she could see the veins beneath her pallid skin, wandered over to them.

"What are their names?" she asked curiously.

"Buckingham, who is in the navy and somewhere at sea, Warwick, who is an adjutant to Wellington, and the youngest one is Huntington, a most outrageous rascal. He's at Harrow with my boy. Hunt Bromney set the headmaster's coat on fire one day, and nearly burned down the entire school. As for the other things he's got up to, they are too numerous to mention."

"Like his brother's lovers," Mrs. Ponsonby said slyly.

"Why was the boy not expelled?" Miss Pale exclaimed.

"The duke has too much wealth and too many influential friends," Lady Percy replied.

"If I were a vicious person," Mrs. Ponsonby said with a vicious little smile, "I would caution Lady Bodenham to set a guard outside Lady Mary's door."

"I don't think a single guard would stop the duke, if he were determined to enter," Lady Smurston noted.

Mrs. Ponsonby's nasty smile grew as she looked at Verity. "Forgive us if we shock you, but perhaps we don't...." She let her sneering words trail off as she shrugged her grub-white shoulders.

"I have heard of the duke and his reputation, as well as certain other bits of gossip that some people apparently feel it necessary for all the world to know," Verity replied with more than a hint of defensive spirit. "However, I should point out that if you believe the duke's attentions to Lady Mary are not honorable, you should be warning her, not us."

Before Mrs. Ponsonby could close her gaping mouth, Lady Smurston colored. "Shh! He's coming this way," she whispered.

"Who?" Verity inquired with forced serenity

even as she felt the duke approach, as if he were encompassed by an aura.

Swallowing hard, Verity didn't move until Eloise appeared at her elbow, the duke in tow.

"I believe you've already been introduced to everyone here, Your Grace," Eloise said, "except for Mrs. Davis-Jones."

Verity had no choice except to turn to him and curtsy.

"Your Grace, allow me to present Mrs. Davis-Jones. Mrs. Davis-Jones, the Duke of Deighton."

"I am pleased to make your acquaintance, Your Grace," Verity replied as etiquette demanded.

His gaze held hers as if he were attempting to mesmerize her. This close, she could see the flecks of gold in his remarkable eyes. The last time she had seen them this close, she had thought their golden tints the reflection of the light from the glowing candle, the same light that made his naked flesh look as if it glowed, too.

He reached out and took her gloved hand. For a horrifying yet thrilling moment, she thought he was actually going to kiss her palm—an outrageously intimate thing to do in company.

Fortunately, he merely brushed her knuckles with his lips.

Even then, her heart raced and her whole body warmed, with both excitement and embarrassment.

"Ah, Mrs. Davis-Jones, I understand that you

are an expert on marital bliss,'' he remarked with blatant and arrogant sarcasm as he raised his eyes to look at her.

She would not be upset. She would not show anything except mild interest as she withdrew her hand. ''I fear the duke is mistaken. I am not an expert on anything.''

Eloise glanced from one to the other, her fan fluttering about her chest. Could it be that Eloise felt as warm as she? Verity wondered.

Indeed, she would not be surprised if every woman in the room was warmed simply by the excitement engendered by the duke's virile presence.

''It seems my dear cousin has finally decided to settle down and marry,'' Eloise announced.

The other ladies couldn't have looked more taken aback if he had suddenly declared a burning desire to become a circus performer.

''It's true, it's true,'' the duke said with a sigh, and a twinkle of mockery in his eyes. ''I have decided to put my neck in the matrimonial noose, like so many others before me.'' He faced Verity. ''Lady Bodenham tells me you and your husband were devoted to each other, even though he was much older than you. Well, I suppose one must take what one can get in the marriage mart.''

In the face of such blatant insolence, Verity's shoulders straightened and her chin lifted a little.

"I loved my husband, though he was indeed considerably older than I."

"Of course. All widows claim they loved their husbands."

"Are you accusing me of lying, Your Grace?"

The tips of the Duke of Deighton's ears reddened. "I would never accuse a lady of deliberately lying."

"Perhaps this is a subject we should not pursue," Miss Pale murmured tentatively.

The duke ignored her and it seemed he recovered quickly from her reminder that it was not in the best of taste to speak of marriage to a widow, for he immediately said, "I confess myself fascinated with married life and marital bliss. Would you say disparity of age is a good thing, then?"

She would not let him bait her. Good God, had she not learned at an early age to ignore those who would taunt her? "I was not aware that love paid heed to age."

"We all pay heed to age."

"Apparently some more than others." She cocked her head and regarded him pensively. "Is it your intention to marry without love? In that case, perhaps we should hear what the Duke of Deighton would consider necessary to ensure matrimonial happiness without love."

"Based upon observation, I would say similarity of station, similarity of interests and—" he grinned with what looked like pure deviltry "—similarity of age."

"It occurs to me that the duke must be most familiar with unhappy marriages, for it would seem my late husband and I are the exception to your rules, and we were very happy until death took him from me."

She let the awkward silence last a moment before continuing. "Of course, marriages without love are the common thing among the nobility, are they not?"

"I do not think the dear duke need worry about that," Lady Smurston interjected with a simper. "Women are all too anxious to fall in love with him."

"Or to make love with me, at any rate."

As all the ladies save Verity looked scandalized, Eloise swatted her cousin with her fan. "Galen! Such talk!"

"Forgive me, Eloise," he said without a hint of contrition.

Verity hoped the duke would decide this was an appropriate time to move on, but instead, he again fastened his intense, sardonic gaze upon her. "Davis-Jones? That is a Welsh name, is it not?"

"My late husband was Welsh."

"Indeed? Then a fine singer, too, no doubt."

"Yes."

"Love songs, I suppose?"

What was he getting at? "Sometimes."

"Do you sing, too?"

His lips curved up into a smile that seemed to entice her beyond all measure to lie and say that she did. "No, Your Grace."

He arched a brow. "No?"

"No."

"A pity." He turned to Eloise. "Does Lady Mary sing?"

"Of course. As I said, she is very accomplished."

"I thought so." He faced the ladies, including Verity. "If you will be so kind as to excuse me, I shall endeavor to persuade Lady Mary to demonstrate her accomplishments."

He sauntered toward the wealthy, titled young lady who, it seemed, was definitely the object of his pursuit and who blushed furiously when she realized he was approaching her.

"I do not think music is all he has in mind," Mrs. Ponsonby sneered.

Verity was very glad they were leaving in the morning. She wouldn't have to endure these gossiping women—or anyone else—anymore.

Chapter Three

Galen told himself he would prefer to forget Verity Escombe had ever existed. After all, whatever they had shared once had been little enough, and long ago, and it had never been affection.

Despite this resolution, he couldn't prevent himself from wondering when and how the shy, awestruck girl had become the vibrant, defiant woman able to give him his due in a verbal battle, and even send him from the field in embarrassed confusion? Gad, it had been years since anybody had made him wish he had spoken differently, about anything.

Perhaps marriage had been the making of her, and if so, she must indeed have been happily, fortunately wed—a truly rare thing in this world, he knew.

"Poor Mrs. Davis-Jones," Lady Mary noted as

she followed Galen's gaze. "I gather she was quite pretty in her day."

Lady Mary's voice held no malice; nevertheless, he turned to regard her with grave intensity.

She flushed with embarrassment and put her hand to the gold chain at her slender throat. "What is it? Is something wrong?"

"Not a thing," Galen replied. It would not be polite to reveal that he was trying to determine how bad Lady Mary's eyesight was, for if Verity was pretty in her youth, she was beautiful now, with the fullness of motherhood to round out her slender body, and an unmistakable, intriguing confidence.

"Your Grace, would you care to join me at the pianoforte?" Lady Mary asked. "Lady Bodenham has some excellent duets. I am sure there must be one you and I both know."

While she waited for his answer, she smiled tremulously, as if speaking to him were a great act of bravery on her part.

It was a reaction he encountered all too frequently. In his youth, it had been a stimulating compliment. Now he found it tiresome.

"Alas, I fear I am no singer," he replied truthfully.

Not like Verity's Welsh husband.

He wondered if little Jocelyn had inherited her father's voice, for the Welsh were notable singers.

She must have her father's dark hair. Those glossy black curls did not come from Verity.

"Perhaps you could turn the pages for me while I play?" Lady Mary suggested.

If her smile had not been so guileless, he might have suspected that Lady Mary was not ignorant of the fact that if he stood beside her while she played, her cleavage, such as it was, would be on display.

Well, why not turn her pages? He had nothing else with which to occupy his time, and he had meant what he said to Eloise. He had returned to England determined to wed, and Lady Mary was not the worst matrimonial prospect he had met.

After escorting her to the piano, Lady Mary began to perform.

For once it seemed that Eloise had not exaggerated when it came to a young woman's accomplishments. Lady Mary had a rich soprano voice and excellent expression, and she played very well, too. Unlike several other ladies Galen could think of, she didn't seem to choose her music with the ulterior motive of impressing him with her knowledge of Italian or German. Lady Mary sang "Flow Gently, Sweet Afton," and she sang it both gently and sweetly, as it ought to be sung.

There was only one thing lacking, he realized, and that was any hint of emotional involvement on the part of the singer.

When she finished, she looked at him expectantly.

"That was lovely," he said. "Will you favor us with another? Perhaps something happier, to fit my mood?"

She smiled brightly and immediately launched into a lively air about spring, children playing and lambs cavorting. She played so energetically, he almost expected her to fall off the seat.

The remarkable speed with which she played made it harder for him to let his attention wander during her selection, but it did nonetheless. He wondered what Verity and Eloise were talking about so seriously in the corner. Him, perhaps? Was Eloise making excuses for him again?

No, it must be something else entirely, for he rarely saw Eloise look so disappointed.

He dutifully turned a page, then he happened to glance at the large, ornate mirror over the mantel.

Good God.

He stared at his reflection as if seeing it for the first time: the dark hair curling about his forehead; the line of his chin to which he had never paid particular heed unless he were shaving; the shape of his nose.

That surprised, wary expression.

How old was Jocelyn? Had anybody said?

She could be ten years old.

His hair? His chin?

His child?

No, surely not! It couldn't be. Verity would have...what? Come sobbing to him claiming he had despoiled her? Followed him to Italy to demand a marriage?

Given the man he was, he could imagine why she would not.

Which did not absolve her from keeping such a secret from him. If he had fathered a child, he should know.

He realized Lady Mary had paused and turned the page herself. "Forgive me," he murmured, smiling at her with his very best smile. He touched a curl on the side of her head. "I was...distracted."

Lady Mary blushed from the top of her breasts to her forehead.

Frowning with frustration, Galen strode into the bedroom Eloise had given over to his use during his visit. Like all the rooms in Eloise's home, this one was decorated with the best furnishings money could buy, if not the best taste. The furniture was massive, and massively ugly, while the color scheme of lime green and gold was nearly enough to make him squint.

"You may retire, Rhodes," Galen said to his waiting valet.

He tried not to betray any impatience, or any

sign that he felt as if his world had suddenly been forever altered. He could hardly have chased after Verity when she left the drawing room before dinner.

And he could be wrong about Jocelyn. Indeed, he had spent the better part of the evening convincing himself any similarity of feature could be mere coincidence.

His portly valet looked as hurt as only Rhodes could. He chewed his lip like a dismayed child before he spoke. "Retire, Your Grace? Now? Before you're in bed?"

"Yes, Rhodes. Now. I think I am quite capable of undressing myself unassisted," Galen replied.

"Your Grace," Rhodes began with dignity, his Cockney origins becoming more in evidence, "I must point out that you'll probably toss your clothes about and then I shall have more of a job making them presentable. I have already had quite a time with the grass stains. I really think you should reconsider."

"Rhodes, I promise I shall not throw my clothes onto the floor or over a chair, and there is no danger of grass stains here."

Rhodes's expression grew rather conniving. "Is there, perhaps, a lady…?"

"As much as I know it disappoints you, given the exciting life you no doubt thought I would lead when I engaged you upon my return to London, no, there is no lady. There is no gambling, there is no drinking, there is no cockfighting, bearbaiting or whoring, either. In short, Rhodes, my life is as dull as a man's could be, and tonight, I intend to read.'' Galen gave his manservant a very pointed look. ''Good night.''

Rhodes became mobile, albeit barely. He headed toward the door, looking as if he expected to be informed this was some kind of outrageous joke and he the butt of it. ''You're going to sit up and read the *Times?*''

''If you find that so surprising, I could always dismiss you, I suppose.''

Rhodes recoiled, then hurried out the door as if pursued by demons. ''Good night, Your Grace! Enjoy the *Times!*''

With a sound between a sigh and a chuckle, Galen closed the door behind his fleeing valet, then glanced at the ornate clock on the mantelpiece. Nearly midnight.

He strolled toward the windows, which looked over the spacious lawn and winding drive leading to Eloise's manor. The moonlight shone brightly, illuminating the scene with only the occasional shadow of a cloud. He could smell the damp in the air, hinting at rain to come.

This view was very different from the one out his bedroom when he had visited Lord Langley in Yorkshire. There, the house had been nestled in a valley in a vain attempt to shield it from the winds and rain that blew across the dales.

The wind had been blowing that night ten years ago, making the single tree near the house moan as it bent and swayed.

At least he thought it had been the tree. Perhaps it had been himself moaning, for quite a different reason.

Staring unseeing out the window, he remembered the events of that night as he had a thousand times before.

After an evening spent with the utterly boring Lord Langley and barely noticing the shy miss who had sat in the corner like a mouse expecting him to pounce, for once not half-drunk, he had been awakened by the soft sound of his door opening. Then came the glow of a single candle's flame.

There had been something almost supernatural about that glow that made him sit up straight. He ignored the chill of the air upon his naked chest, which rose and fell with his rapid breathing.

Holding the candle, her long brown hair unbound, and wearing a simple white nightdress, Verity came into his room.

He would have been only slightly less surprised if she had been a ghost. He wondered if she walked in her sleep, and he waited to see what she would do. He had heard it was not wise to wake someone in that state, and given that she held a candle, he didn't want to startle her and make her drop it upon her thin nightdress.

It was very thin, so thin he could see her rosy nipples clearly, and the darker triangle lower down. A simple drawstring at the neck was all the closing it had. One pull, and it would loosen and fall.

She came straight to his bed and set the candle down on the table beside him before looking directly at him.

He knew immediately that she was as wide-awake as he.

Completely taken aback, he started to speak— but she leaned toward him and laid one slender finger against his lips. Then she gently traced their outline.

It was a simple gesture, yet one that had set his blood pounding fiercely in his veins, firing his desire more than another woman's boldest caress.

He could smell the light perfume of her naked skin mingling with the candle's wax and see how her nightgown grew taut over her unexpectedly voluptuous breasts.

When she moved back, he felt a loss as great as another might for a fortune sunk to the bottom of the sea—until she pulled the drawstring, then tugged the nightdress lower.

And lower. Soon it was a discarded heap on the floor.

Wordlessly, wonderingly, he held out his hands

and helped the lithe beauty into his bed. They said not a single word as they began to caress each other.

No word need be said, for it was as if he had waited all his life for her to be in his arms. Guided only by her soft breathing and low moans, he gave pleasure, and received it.

Never before or since had he felt as worthy and desirable and irresistible as Verity Escombe made him feel that night. No act of love had ever been as exciting, or as sweet.

When she parted her legs for him, he gently pushed into her with barely suppressed urgency, until he encountered the barrier of her maidenhead.

Suddenly uncertain, he hesitated—until she pulled him closer and wrapped her legs around him, drawing him further inside.

He needed no more reassurance or encouragement. Moving as if they were one body, their panting breaths mingling, the climax was not long delayed.

Afterward, when he was sweat slicked, sated and satisfied beyond measure, she lay still beneath him, breathing softly.

Enveloped by a tenderness he had not known he possessed, he whispered her name and reached out for her.

Only to have her scramble from the bed. She tugged on her nightgown and ran from the room.

Despite his pleas to tell him what was the matter, she had left him.

As if he carried the plague.

For ten years, he had wondered what had brought her to his bedroom and into his arms.

For ten years, he had tried to convince himself it didn't matter. He had commanded himself to forget what had happened and told himself his act of love had no serious consequences, for either of them.

He knew better now, and this time, he would not let Verity run away without an explanation.

"Mama?"

Verity sat up. Jocelyn stood uncertainly on the threshold of the doorway between their bedchambers.

"What is it?" Verity asked softly.

She sucked in her breath when her bare feet touched the cold parquet floor, then hurried to Jocelyn. Crouching down to her level, she put her arms around her daughter. "Are you ill? Did you have a bad dream?"

For weeks after Daniel's death, Jocelyn had had nightmares. She had not been so troubled for some time, but perhaps the upheaval of travel had brought them back—another good reason to return home.

Jocelyn shook her head. "I woke up when you came to bed and now I can't get back to sleep."

"Oh." Verity took her daughter's hand and led her to her huge bed with its heavy curtains and slippery satin sheets. "Were you cold?"

"A little."

"Climb up and snuggle with me, then," Verity said, cuddling under the expensive coverings beside her daughter. "There. Is this not better?"

Jocelyn nodded.

"You will sleep well again when we're back home."

"Will you sing to me, Mama?"

"Gladly, little girl, gladly," she answered with a smile full of love.

"The one about the three ships, Mama," Jocelyn replied with a yawn.

Quietly Verity sang her daughter's favorite song until her eyes closed and the slow rising and falling of her chest told her she was asleep.

How young Jocelyn looked when she slept, more like a toddler again, with her damp curls and dark eyelashes fanning on her smooth cheeks!

Did the duke look young when he slept, too? Verity wondered. Somehow, she thought he would, and that perhaps in sleep she would see even more of a resemblance between her daughter and her natural father.

That thought made her more determined to flee

than ever, before anybody else noticed how much Jocelyn looked like the duke.

She decided she should carry Jocelyn back to her own bed, or Nancy would be shocked into a panic when she awoke and found her charge's bed empty.

Verity got up, slipped on her shoes and again regarded her innocent child, the living memory of her passionate night with a man she barely knew. As always, she felt shame and remorse at the thought of her lustful selfishness. If disaster fell upon her and her child, she would only have herself to blame.

Yet every time she cursed herself for her selfishness, she thought of Jocelyn, too, whom she would not have but for the duke. Because of Jocelyn, she could not be completely sorry for what she had done.

She gently lifted her daughter and tried to carry her to the other room without waking her. That wasn't easy, given Jocelyn's size, but she managed it, and got her into bed without waking Nancy, either.

Pleased with her success, she returned to her bedroom, closed the connecting door, turned—and collided with Galen Bromney.

He grabbed hold of her shoulders as she stumbled backward.

How well she remembered the strength of his

fingers, the feel of his hands on her body, the desire to be held in his powerful arms—memories that she *must* conquer.

Panting slightly, she twisted away from him and struggled to regain her composure.

"Go away!" she ordered quietly, mindful that Nancy and Jocelyn were only a few feet away.

The hard angles of his face shone in the moonlight as if he were some kind of demonic specter come to haunt her. "That's not a very polite greeting, considering what we've been to each other."

She sidled away from the door and away from the duke. "We were very little to each other, I think."

"Ah, you sadly underestimate yourself, Verity," he replied, his voice low and seductive as his intense gaze followed her. "I remember nearly everything about that night, especially the way you left me. Then you departed Lord Langley's before I came down for breakfast."

As tempting as it was to make him understand why she had left as she had, what good would it do?

"Please leave, Your Grace. You mustn't be discovered here," she said, suddenly very aware that she was wearing only her nightdress.

"Because you don't want anybody to know I am Jocelyn's father."

The color draining from her face, Verity stared at him.

"It's true, isn't it?" Galen continued inexorably as he came closer to her. "Her age would be right, and she resembles me."

Verity sidestepped him and crossed the room. "Please leave, Your Grace."

"I have a right to know if the child is mine, Verity."

"Go," she pleaded in a whisper, "and I will tell you all in the morning."

"Tell me now."

"It is late—"

"It is indeed late for me to know if she is mine."

He moved toward her. "She is, isn't she?" he asked in a whisper as he reached out and took her again by the shoulders. "You don't have to tell me. I know she is."

He pulled her into his embrace, and she tried to remember why this was wrong. "A stronger, finer man would have sent you from his bedroom that night. Unfortunately, I was weak." His voice dropped to a sultry whisper. "You make me weak. Even now."

Then he kissed her.

Despite his words, there was nothing weak about his kiss. Just as before, on that long-ago night, his lips took hers with passionate possession, demanding that she surrender to his power and give in to her desire.

How tempting he was! How dangerously, sinfully tempting...

But she had learned the consequences of giving in to such dangerous temptation.

She broke the kiss and pushed him away. "Please, Your Grace, go. I will explain tomorrow."

That was another lie. She would sooner march into a den of starving lions than meet the Duke of Deighton alone.

His expression hardened. "I perceive that whatever attraction I held for you in the past is quite finished."

"I was young and foolish then."

"Gad, madam, so was I." He bowed with stiff formality. "It will be as you wish. We will speak again in the morning. Meet me in the library at, say, nine o'clock? I daresay it will be deserted. Eloise's guests are not generally the sort to read."

Nine o'clock. After they had gone.

Desperate to be away from him, she nodded eagerly, then hurried to the door and peered into the corridor. "It is safe to go now."

She felt him come behind her and quickly stepped aside to let him pass. As he did, he briefly touched her hand.

Her breath caught in her throat even as she

steeled herself to order him to go. She would not look into his fascinating eyes.

She would charge him not to kiss her again.

But in the next instant, he was gone.

Galen dressed in the faint light of dawn without his valet's assistance. Not wanting to disturb anyone and not hungry in the least, he immediately went to wait in the library, which was as silent as his villa on a Sunday afternoon.

He would read, which was how he usually spent his silent Sundays. He scanned the shelves and finally decided on a volume of Shakespeare's sonnets. However, when he opened the book, he discovered that damp and more than one insect had been at work, more proof if he required it that the books in Eloise's library were more for decoration than literary enjoyment.

He closed the book, returned it to its place and paced, with frequent glances at the gold clock on the mantel, which was so ornate it was not easy to tell the time the first few times he looked. However, it got easier.

What was he going to say to Verity? he pondered. He must be firm, for he was determined to hear the truth from her own lips. Yet he must not be too harsh, not if he wanted to know more about his daughter, and to see her again. He would ruin any chance of that if he frightened Verity, and he knew he could be very frightening when angry.

He decided just how he would begin, and the tone he would use, and at last nine o'clock came.

And went.

He gave her fifteen minutes. Fifteen minutes during which he tried to believe she had not deserted him again, and that he had not been a fool to trust her.

Fifteen minutes to anticipate her arrival. To be annoyed and then hopeful, then annoyed again. To try to command his emotions so that he wouldn't upset her or give her any cause to flee.

After that long fifteen minutes, Galen strode into the hall and commandeered the first liveried footman he spied. "I'd like you to take a message to Mrs. Davis-Jones."

"Mrs. Davis-Jones?" the young man repeated stupidly.

"Yes, Mrs. Davis-Jones."

"But Your Grace, um," the fellow stammered, looking down as if feeling a sudden need to count the buttons of his purple jacket. "She's gone, Your Grace."

"Gone?" Galen growled.

"Aye, Your Grace, left this morning at six o'clock, Mrs. Davis-Jones, her little girl and that minx of a servant, too."

"Thank you," Galen said evenly as he returned to the library and shut the door behind him.

He strode to the window and stared out unseeing at Eloise's garden and the shrubbery beyond.

Verity had done it again, damn her. She had run away like a thief in the night, without explanation or any concern for him at all.

He had not gone after her ten years ago. This time, though, things were different.

This time, he had a most excellent reason to go after Verity.

And her name was Jocelyn.

Chapter Four

The hired carriage rolled to a stop outside Verity's house.

They had disembarked the post chaise at Jefford, a village of five hundred souls in Warwickshire, and hired the innkeeper's lad and carriage to take them to their house, located a short way beyond the village and down a secluded lane.

"Well, here we are, safe and sound, although my back may never be the same," Nancy declared. "I swear them chaises get smaller all the time."

"Or you're getting bigger," Jocelyn proposed.

Nancy glanced at her sharply, but a sudden lurch of the vehicle turned her attention to the innkeeper's son, a tall fellow who seemed all arms and legs and slouching posture, as if he were a sleepy spider.

"Watch it, there, you nit!" Nancy snapped, her command making Jocelyn giggle and Verity give her friend a mildly chastising look. They had discussed Nancy's language before, with mixed results. At least this time, her choice of chastisement was relatively minor.

With a rueful shrug, Nancy gathered up her skirts and proceeded to climb out, while Verity ran a fond gaze over her comfortable, half-timbered house. Daniel had been a prosperous wool merchant who used local weavers working in their own cottages to manufacture very fine quality goods. He had purchased this home for her before they were married.

Daniel had possessed a more gregarious nature than she at that time in her life, yet he had kindly accepted her desire to live outside the village, away from prying, if well-meaning, neighbors.

She had always loved this house's extra privacy, for it was well hidden from the road and surrounded by a stone wall, as well as tall oak and chestnut trees. A small wood complete with babbling stream ran across the back of the property.

The leaves of the chestnut trees were turning golden, and the beeches were reddening. Jocelyn would be able to pick elderberries soon, and mushrooms, too. Verity could hear finches singing in the trees, and the harsh caw of a rook in the distance.

Adjoining her land was the large estate of Sir Myron Thorpe, a man of about thirty whose primary interest in life seemed to be hunting and fishing. They were nodding acquaintances only, for Verity did not much care to go about in company, and his company seemed primarily composed of men anyway.

As much as Verity loved the house, so did Jocelyn. Shortly after Daniel's death, Verity had tentatively suggested moving into the town, only to see her daughter dissolve into sobs at the very notion. Truth be told, Verity had been relieved, for she did not want to leave her secure seclusion, either.

"Visiting is all very well," Verity said with a sigh as she reached up to help Jocelyn down, "but there's nothing like home, when all is said and done."

"I'm hungry," her daughter announced as she set foot on the drive.

"I'll get you something while Nancy deals with the baggage," Verity replied as she took Jocelyn's hand to lead her into the house.

From outside, all seemed exactly as they had left it.

But when she put her hand on the latch of the heavy carved door, she realized it was already open.

Trying to remain calm, she let go of Jocelyn's hand and stepped back warily. "Will you please ask Nancy if she needs any assistance?" she said, smiling at her daughter.

"But —"

"Please, Jocelyn."

Frowning, Jocelyn did as her mother asked.

When she had turned and gone back down the steps, Verity slowly pushed open the door and peered cautiously into the front entryway.

"Why, my dear Verity, here you are!" Clive Blackstone cried as he appeared at the entrance to her parlor, his lips drawn back in a smile over his crooked front teeth.

Verity would have been happier to encounter a housebreaker, or even the Duke of Deighton, than her obsequious brother-in-law.

"Yes, here you are," Daniel's sister, Fanny, quietly echoed from behind him.

Her thin body shrouded in a dark gray cloak, and with her pale face and large, cowlike eyes, she looked like a wraith in the shadows, a distinct contrast to her gaudily attired husband. Clive wore a mustard-colored jacket, burgundy waistcoat with a gold pattern upon it and striped brown trousers. A bulging valise was at his feet.

"We came to visit and were shocked to realize you were not at home," the towheaded, middle-aged Clive said as he waited for Verity to approach.

As if this were his house, not hers.

Despite her annoyance, she forced a smile onto

her face. "I'm sorry we were not here when you arrived," she said evenly.

She always forced herself to speak calmly when she was with the Blackstones, especially since Daniel's death. She would give them no cause to quarrel with her. "However did you manage to get inside?"

"Oh, did you not know we had a key? Dear Daniel was good enough to give Fanny one before he passed away. We never had occasion to use it before, but fortunately, we brought it with us."

Verity continued to smile. "I trust you have not been waiting long," she said, glancing at the cloaked Fanny.

"Not at all. We walked up from the inn and arrived only a few moments ago. Had we known the situation, we would have waited for you there."

And come in their carriage, for which *she* paid, Verity thought grimly. Still, she wouldn't have minded so much, for Fanny's sake. She looked exhausted.

There had been no need for them to walk, in any event. Clive could afford the hire of a carriage as well as she, no matter how much money he claimed to have invested in his cotton mills. He was just too much of a miser to spare his wife the walk.

"If you had written to apprise me of your intentions beforehand—"

"Nancy doesn't want any help," Jocelyn declared from the front door.

Glad of the interruption, for otherwise she might have said something regrettable, Verity turned to see her obviously dismayed daughter in the doorway. She gave her a pointed look and smiled all the more, a definite hint to her daughter to be polite to their guests. *Any* guests, no matter how unwelcome. "Say hello to Uncle Clive and Aunt Fanny, Jocelyn."

"Hello, Uncle Clive," Jocelyn said obediently, and without enthusiasm. "Hello, Aunt Fanny."

"Please go to your room and take off your cloak and bonnet. Then you may help Nancy unpack your things when she comes."

Jocelyn nodded, all the joy of their return ruined for her, as it was for her mother.

"This is indeed most fortuitous," Clive continued as Jocelyn slowly walked up the stairs on the right of the entry. "I was just saying we would have to go to the Jefford Arms for accommodation, wasn't I, Fanny?"

His wife nodded.

A loud and distinctly disdainful sniff from the front door drew their attention.

Nancy stood on the threshold, one small trunk

under each arm, and a bandbox in her hand, glaring at Clive and his wife malevolently.

Verity hurried toward her. Her back was to Clive and Fanny, so they couldn't see her expression, which was both determined and pleading. "Look who has come!"

"I see. Them."

"Nancy, please!" Verity whispered.

With a resigned glance at her mistress, Nancy put an expression on her face that was supposed to be a smile, although it was far more like a grimace than anything else.

"How do you do, Mr. Blackstone, Mrs. Blackstone?" she inquired with cold civility.

Before they could answer, she briskly continued, going up the stairs after Jocelyn. "Well, enough chitchat. I've got to get to work. Mustn't malinger. Mustn't stand about like I'm the emperor of China with all the time in the world to chat and run about visiting folks."

"If you'll excuse me a moment, I'd like to take off my traveling clothes," Verity said hastily as she hurried after Nancy without waiting for a response from her in-laws.

"Those crows always come any old time it suits them," Nancy muttered as she reached the landing and turned toward the upper floor. "Think this is an hotel, they do, with all their coming and going, and him supposed to be in business. My eye! If he is, he'll soon be bankrupt!''

Verity let Nancy mutter until they entered Verity's bedchamber at the front of the house. She closed the door as Nancy put down the trunks. "Nancy, I must ask you again to please *try* to speak to the Blackstones with some respect."

"I do try. I just ain't very good at it," Nancy confessed as she faced her mistress.

Verity began to untie the ribbons of her plain black bonnet. "Please, you *must* try harder. They are my relations, after all, and I must ask you to respect my wishes."

Nancy sighed with the sorrow of the ages. "For you, I'll do me best—but I can't promise to do more. They make my flesh crawl!"

"You know I do not like them either, yet we must be nice to them, for Daniel's sake, and Jocelyn's, too," Verity continued as she removed her pelisse. "They are the only relations we have, after all."

"And blood is thicker than water," Nancy said, and sighed as if they had had this conversation many times before as, in fact, they had.

"Yes. Jocelyn can hear how you speak to them, you know, and you influence her a great deal. Unfortunately, if anything were to happen to me, they would be her guardians, so we must take care to ensure that she does not upset them."

"Aye, I know," Nancy admitted remorsefully, "and I'll try harder, really I will."

Verity smiled. "I know. Now will you please go and see what Jocelyn is up to? She need not come downstairs at once, if she doesn't want to."

"I daresay she won't," Nancy said, "but I'll do my best to persuade her."

"Thank you, Nancy."

"How long do you think they've come for this time?"

"I saw only a small valise, so perhaps this will be a short sojourn."

"I hope to heaven you're right!" Nancy declared with a brusque nod as she headed for the door. "Or I'll probably bust a stay trying to keep me thoughts to meself."

When she had gone, Verity rotated her neck, already feeling the tension Clive always engendered.

It seemed she had left one anxiety-inducing scene for another—but at least this one she was familiar with and she knew how to conduct herself.

Nevertheless, Verity would have preferred to hide upstairs, too, until Clive and Fanny got annoyed and left, but as that would be altogether too rude, she could only linger for a few moments to tidy her hair.

"Oh, shut that mouth of yours and stop whining!" Clive commanded his wife in a harsh whisper. He ran his finger along the marbled mantelpiece, stopping when he touched the heavy silver candlestick. "We're here and we're not leaving until I say so."

"But, my love—" Fanny began as she hovered near the door.

Clive's mouth twisted with anger and disgust. "Are you such an idiot you can't remember one thing I say? I'm sure there's more to her visit to that woman than a change of scene."

"What else—?"

"Something," Clive said darkly. "And I want to know what."

Fanny wanted to weep, but Clive hated it when she wept, so she turned away and surreptitiously wiped her tears before they fell.

As she did, she wished again that Verity's father had never met her brother, Daniel. Then, when Verity's wastrel father had died penniless, her kindhearted brother would not have taken it upon himself to look after Verity. He would not have married her and spent all that money on this lovely house, so much finer than the one she shared with Clive.

Her gaze roved over the walls painted a pale sea green, the fine floral brocade of the sofa and drapes, Daniel's portrait over the mantel, the silver candlesticks that she knew Clive coveted as if they were solid gold, and finally the thick, luxurious carpet upon which she stood.

In her wildest dreams Fanny had never supposed her placid brother would marry Verity Escombe, whose family's lost wealth came from a source that filled him with repugnance, or that there would be a child who would take away her inheritance.

She knew Clive had not expected it, either.

"What are you doing hunched over like that?" Clive demanded querulously. "Stand up straight, can't you?"

She did as he commanded.

"Here she comes. Now for heaven's sake, smile. And try to find out why she really went to Lady Bodenham's."

"Yes, Clive."

Unfortunately for Fanny, Verity had gone to Eloise's solely for a friendly visit and no other reason. As for any other subject, such as the unexpected arrival of the Duke of Deighton, Jocelyn never spoke of him, and Verity had ten long years of practice when it came to keeping secrets.

A fortnight later, sitting in a leather-covered wing chair, surrounded by books he had never read and pictures he never noticed, his favorite dogs at his feet, Sir Myron Thorpe nodded off over a brandy. It had been a long, boring day, and he would be a happy man once he had some company for the hunting season.

Yawning prodigiously, he moved to pick up another piece of pineapple from the plate at his elbow when he happened to look out his study window.

He abruptly straightened, as alert as a hound—something he rather resembled—catching the scent of a hare. His awakened dogs lifted their heads and sniffed the air.

"Charles, my telescope," he cried to an elderly servant who was making a halfhearted attempt to clean the hearth.

While Charles got up as quickly as his creaking knees would let him and tottered toward the tall secretary desk to find the instrument, Myron commanded his now alert dogs to sit, tossed the piece of pineapple into his mouth and went to the window.

He didn't wait to swallow before addressing Charles again. "Maybe it isn't him, after all. I've invited him here every year since we left Harrow. I've just about given up hope."

Charles found the telescope and brought it to Sir Myron, who held it to his eye. Then he nearly dropped it. "Good God, it *is* the Duke of Deighton, as I live and breathe. And just look at that horse. Where the devil does he find 'em? I'd give six of mine for that one."

"Might the gentleman be staying to tea?"

Charles asked, quite used to his master's mode of communication, which was inevitably loud and enthusiastic.

"Tea? Galen Bromney coming to *tea?* Are you mad? No, he's finally taken up my invitation to hunt with me. Why else would he come?"

"Ah. Then I had best inform Mrs. Minnigan."

"Of course you should inform the housekeeper! At once! She should prepare the best rooms for him."

"Very good, sir," Charles intoned as he made a little bow and left the room.

Myron tossed his telescope onto the nearest chair, grabbed his tweed jacket and hurried outside to the wide steps fronting his house, trailed by his excited dogs who no doubt anticipated another foray after rabbits or deer.

"Gad, I haven't seen Deighton in, what, fifteen years?" he muttered in an excited soliloquy. "Bit of a ladies' man after Harrow according to Justbury Minor, but none the worse for it! My God, look at his seat. Perfect! I suppose his man is coming with his things later. Ho there!"

Galen could not have missed Myron if he wanted to. It was ever thus, from the first day they were at school. Myron's voice was, by some quirk of nature, loud even when he whispered, which meant he could never be included in the plans of the more daring schoolboys. Nor was he at all capable of deceit; indeed, Galen could well believe dishonesty simply did not exist within Myron's trusting and honest nature. Unfortunately, that also meant Myron was often treated like the village idiot until Galen had befriended him, something for which Myron had been rather pathetically grateful. At first, his gratitude had been a nuisance. Then it became enjoyable having such a thankful lackey who could always be counted on to say something admiring.

After he had left school, Galen had almost instantly forgotten all about Myron, until he had learned where Verity lived from the unsuspecting Eloise, and he recalled that his former friend also lived in Jefford. Better yet, Myron invited him to hunt every year, even though Galen had yet to accept the invitation.

As keen as he had been to rush to Jefford the day after Verity had departed Potterton Abbey, he had not. He had learned to govern his impulses better, with the glaring exception of the kiss he had shared with Verity in her bedchamber at Eloise's.

When their lips touched, passion and desire had immediately surged into vibrant life within him, as if he had suddenly been awakened from a long sleep, or as if no time had elapsed since they had last shared a passionate embrace.

It had taken every ounce of his self-control to leave that bedchamber without kissing her again.

Even the simple touch of her hand had kindled more longing within him than he had felt in years.

As he pulled his horse to a halt in front of Myron, who was both smiling up at him and patting the heads of his large hunting dogs, he reflected that there was a time he would not have felt a particle of remorse for using his friend in this manner.

Those days were past, he told himself as he dismounted and went to shake hands with Myron, who was a little heavier than he had been of yore, but otherwise not much altered by the passage of time. He was still tall and brawny, with brown hair untouched by gray, and a florid face.

"Welcome to my humble hunting lodge, Your Grace!" Myron cried happily.

Galen gave the fine stone manor an admiring glance. "Thank you for the invitation, Myron, although not every man would refer to such a splendid abode as a hunting lodge."

Myron blushed like a girl getting her first compliment at a ball. "It's a trifle, really," he said with an attempt at modesty quite undone by his obvious pride. "Someplace to display trophies and keep the guns, that's all."

"If it is possible to have that much good hunting around Jefford, I really should have come much sooner."

Myron roared with laughter and clapped his

hand on Galen's shoulder so hard he winced. "I do what I can to keep the wild population hereabouts under control. You must be parched. Care for a drink?"

"I would be delighted," Galen replied as he followed his host into the front hall, which was decorated with an astonishing array of weaponry. The dogs trotted behind, then wandered off down the corridor.

"You're not expecting a siege, I hope?" Galen inquired as he eyed the various lances, crossbows, arrows, bows, swords and pikes.

"I wasn't before, but I am now!" Myron chortled as he ran an approving gaze over Galen. "Demme, age becomes you, Deighton! You're handsomer than ever. We'll have to fight off the women when they hear you've come."

Galen sighed mournfully as they entered what Galen took to be Myron's study, done in age-darkened oak paneling and decidedly masculine. Portraits of hunting dogs and horses covered the walls, and Galen realized the dogs had been headed here, for they now lounged around one particularly well used chair. Their presence and obvious familiarity with their places no doubt explained the heavy odor of dog in the room.

"Such is the story of my life. Besieged and beleaguered when all I seek is a little sport," Galen replied.

Myron grinned as he poured him a large brandy. "Sport is what some of 'em are after, too, eh?"

Galen could not disagree. "Nevertheless, Myron, I am tired of such empty liaisons. I have decided I should marry, so if you know of any pretty, rich, titled eligible ladies nearby who are in need of a husband, I shall be happy to meet them."

Myron walked toward Galen, unmindfully spilling brandy with every step. As Galen took the glass, he noticed that the once fine Aubusson carpet bore evidence that this sort of genial messiness was not unusual in Myron's study.

"Married? You?" his host demanded.

Galen settled onto the worn sofa and regarded Myron with genial amusement. "I am not repulsive, I hope."

Myron laughed so hard most of his brandy never stood a chance. "Repulsive? The Duke of Deighton? Oh, sink me for a simpleton, that's good!"

"It has been brought to my attention by several well-meaning people that I am not in my youth any longer, and it is high time I took a wife. Therefore, if you have any suggestions, I am all ears."

Myron cleared his throat and a serious expression appeared on his pleasant face. "Well, let me see…there's Lady Alice de Monfrey—but she's too old. And the Duchess of Tewkesbury's daughter—but she looks like a bitch with a sour tooth."

He scratched his chin. "There's Verity Davis-Jones—no, not her."

"What is the matter with her?" Galen inquired lightly.

"She's a widow."

"A rich widow might be the very thing. Or is she ancient?"

Myron let out a snort. "Not at all, but she's not rich or important. Her child stands to inherit a goodly sum when she comes of age, but the mother has only a portion of the income to live on. As for the little girl, she's a hellion!"

"Why, Myron, since when have you taken to listening to school-yard gossip?"

"I don't! She once stampeded a herd of cows through the main street of the village."

Galen subdued a grin. "I find that difficult to believe."

"She said the gate to the pasture was already open, but she was laughing so hard, nobody except her mother and that termagant of a servant believed her."

Galen wondered if he would ever get the chance to ask Jocelyn herself about that. Even if he didn't, he already believed her version of events.

Myron cleared his throat. "And her husband's demise was said to be rather...hasty."

Galen regarded his host with apparently mild interest. "Was it an accident? Is foul play suspected?"

"Not by anybody who ever met the widow. Unthinkable to imagine her up to no good! Yet here he was in perfect health one week, and the next he was dead."

"He was a young man, then?"

"Good God, no. Fifty if he was a day—but healthy for all that."

"What did the doctor say?"

"Pneumonia."

"Is there some cause to believe the doctor would lie?"

Myron shook his head. "Dr. Newton is very well respected in the county. But you know how women gossip! They always will when the husband is so much older than the wife and then shuffles off his mortal coil so quick. I confess I wondered myself at the time—yet only for an instant. I saw them together a few times, and there's no doubt she loved her husband very much. Wouldn't leave him for a day, even when he was well." Myron sighed. "Gad, we should all be so lucky as to have a woman like that tending to us in our final days!"

"You make her sound more like a nurse than a wife."

"I'd settle for a nurse like that, by God!" Myron

cried with a throaty chuckle. "There was the child, too. Demme, that man doted on his daughter!"

"How paternal of him."

Myron gave him a quizzical look, then grinned. "Gad, forgive me! You don't want to hear about widows and their children!"

"I do not want to spend all my time with the fairer sex, either, not when I could be hunting with such a sportsman as yourself. I truly regret not coming sooner, Myron. I have been in Italy."

"Demme, I know that!" Myron declared. "Justbury Minor keeps me informed of all the old boys' doings."

Galen realized he should have guessed this. The younger Justbury boy—hence, minor—was the worst gossip Galen had ever met, male or female. He made Eloise seem a sphinx. What Justbury knew, he told, too.

"Mind, I'll have to have a dinner party or two," Myron mused aloud, "or the ladies will never forgive me."

Galen smiled with appropriate modesty and inclined his head. Then he frowned. "Not tonight, I hope."

"No! Not tonight, or tomorrow either, for the weather promises to be fair. Tomorrow I must take you out for the pheasants. Then fishing—perhaps the ladies will have to wait a little, eh?"

"Whatever you think best, Myron."

"Mind, it's a wonder any young ladies live long enough to be married these days, what with those flimsy dresses and low bodices and whatnot. Asking for consumption, if you ask me!"

"I rather like the current mode in ladies' fashions," Galen noted absently. Even in black, Verity had looked beautiful in her simple gown that revealed the tantalizing tops of her breasts.

"You would, you dog!"

Brought back to the present, Galen raised his glass in a salute. "To your very good health, Myron, and renewed friendships."

Myron flushed and Galen could almost believe the genial soul had a tear in his eye. "I'm so delighted you have come at last, Your Grace. I've missed you."

Galen realized he had robbed himself of something rather precious for too long. "No more of this title nonsense. We are friends, Myron, and there is no need to stand on rank. And I hope you do not mind if I avail myself of your hospitality for a long time, to make up for all the years I have missed."

"Of course, your—Galen. Of course."

Chapter Five

Verity glanced at the letter in her hand. The small, unassuming white sheet of paper with her address written in a plain and simple hand had come in the day's post. She surmised it was from an acquaintance of her late husband who had not heard of his death. Sighing, she gently pried up the unstamped sealing wax.

She glanced at the signature—then blindly felt for the chair behind her, sitting heavily.

Dear Madam,
I trust you are well and that your sudden departure from our mutual friend's was not caused by any serious indisposition. If it was, I sincerely hope you are recovered enough to allow me the pleasure of an interview.

Since we have a common interest, I am

most desirous of meeting with you. I will come after the noon today.

> Yours sincerely,
> Deighton.

The blood throbbed in her ears as her heart pounded wildly.

He was coming here, to her home. Today. Without asking if it was convenient, or giving her any opportunity to refuse to see him.

A "common interest" could only mean Jocelyn.

She couldn't risk the Duke of Deighton coming here. What if somebody saw him? What would they think?

She could always tell a portion of the truth, which was that she had met him at Lady Bodenham's.

That might work with any other nobleman, but not him. Not with his reputation, even after all this time. She was young, she was widowed—people would surely leap to the basest of conclusions.

Then they might look at Jocelyn and guess...

The sound of Jocelyn's giggles reached her from the kitchen, accompanied by Nancy's throaty laughter.

Thank heavens Clive and Fanny had gone home.

The duke must be in Jefford if he was coming this very afternoon. He was either staying with Sir Myron, the only person of rank in the county, or at the Jefford Arms.

Even if she did find out where he was, she could hardly send him a note. That would cause as much gossip as anything else could.

Why did Galen Bromney have to come here? What could he want? What was there to discuss? Jocelyn was her responsibility. She wanted nothing from him, not now and not ever.

Indeed, he could be nothing in their child's life. No one must ever know that Jocelyn was the Duke of Deighton's daughter. She did not want her child to live with the shame and humiliation of being a bastard.

And if Clive discovered her secret, she was sure he would use that information to try to take away Jocelyn's inheritance without a moment of remorse, or a single thought for the pain or hardship he would cause.

Glancing at the clock, Verity tried to calm herself. It was nearly one o'clock. Perhaps the duke had reconsidered.

Then her breath caught in her throat as a horse bearing a very familiar rider appeared in the long drive. She would know that posture anywhere: the proud carriage of his head, the straight back, the air of possessive arrogance.

He must not come into the house! Somehow, she must keep him outside, away from Jocelyn and Nancy.

With that her only thought, she quickly and quietly hurried outside. As she waited for him on the single step, she wrapped her arms around herself. Although the day was chilly and damp, that was not the reason she trembled.

The duke pulled his horse to a stop and looked at her.

Despite her need to make him leave, Verity felt the heated flush of shame and—worse!—shameful desire possessing her. How attractive he was, with his well-tailored riding clothes that emphasized his broad shoulders, narrow waist and muscular thighs! How he seemed to embody masculine virility in every aspect of his form and figure!

How could she be so foolish, after all that had happened? "Your Grace, you should not—"

"Yes, I should," he said firmly as he dismounted. He looked at her again, and she saw the determined resolution in his hazel eyes. "And I assure you, madam, this time I shall not leave until you have answered my questions."

"This is my property, Your Grace, and you are trespassing upon it."

He smiled slowly, knowingly, in a way that made her pulse quicken even more.

She must be strong! She must not let him linger!

"It was my understanding that the property went to your daughter upon your husband's death. Shall I ask Jocelyn if I may stay?"

"No!" she snapped, inwardly cursing Eloise's

gossiping tongue. She should have guessed that what was already known about her business would go from Eloise's lips to Galen's ear. "Bring your horse and come with me."

He nodded his acquiescence, so with brisk, determined steps, she led him around the side of the house farthest from the kitchen to the small carriage house at the back of the yard. She shoved open the heavy, creaking door, hoping no one in the kitchen could hear.

Inside, light streamed through the dusty windows and motes danced about like so many little bits of fairy dust. Although it had not been used since Daniel's death, it still smelled of hay and horse.

Despite her annoyance and trepidation, when the duke entered and she closed the door behind him, she felt as if she were shutting out a world full of gossiping busybodies who would never understand what might compel a young woman to forget about duty and honor for a night of passion in the Duke of Deighton's arms.

As she continued to watch him while he stabled his horse, she thought perhaps some women might.

Indeed, if half the stories Eloise had told her were true, several woman had been similarly tempted.

It did not comfort Verity to think that she had anything in common with the duke's many lovers, and she would not allow herself to be tempted by him again, not even here.

Where they were alone.

He glanced at her as he tied his black stallion in the stall. "Not quite the place I would choose for this conversation, but it will have to do, I fear."

"It must do. Nobody in Jefford knows that I've ever met you."

He regarded her with calm equanimity. "All you need say is that we became acquainted at my cousin's."

Verity clasped her hands together so tightly her knuckles whitened. "Your Grace, I must again ask you to leave."

His lips jerked up in a little smile. "What, no bogus offers to meet again at a later date?" His gaze roved over the unused building, hesitating a moment on the closed door. "A perfect place for a clandestine rendezvous, if rather dusty."

"This is *not* a clandestine rendezvous!"

"More's the pity."

She pursed her lips. "This may be amusing to you, Your Grace, but I assure you a visit from you may have serious repercussions for me if it becomes known."

His expression unexpectedly softened. "I know all about gossip. That is why I came through your charming wood nearly the whole way."

"Thank goodness for that," Verity snapped as

she crossed her arms over her chest, commanding herself not to be moved by the change in his manner.

He should not have invited himself here, he should not be alone with her, and he should not look so...so *kind*.

"However, I was not about to come to the back of the house like a peddler or beggar."

He moved to block the only exit. "I also will not leave here and I won't let you run away until you answer my questions," he reiterated firmly. "The first thing I must know is, is Jocelyn my daughter?"

As the Duke of Deighton stood before her, his whole body braced as if expecting a blow, Verity saw the fierce determination in his hazel eyes. If that had been all she saw, she might have lied to him.

Yet there was more, a pleading, anxious look, a vulnerability she recognized and that touched her soul. If she lied to him now, she would be doing more than hiding the truth from him. She would be stealing something precious and wonderful.

Slowly she nodded her head. "Yes."

As he let out his breath, Verity straightened her shoulders with renewed determination. "That is why you cannot come here again. There is a resemblance. Anybody seeing the two of you together may guess the truth, and we cannot risk that.''

"I could recite the names of several acquaintances who are bastards, whether most people know it or not," he said. "Once the heir is assured, such…lapses…are not uncommon.''

"Perhaps among the nobility, but we are not of that class. It is also different for a man. Indeed, illegitimate children are more often considered proof of virility.''

"I know society has several standards of acceptable behavior depending upon wealth and rank and sex.''

"You have been protected all your life by your money and status, Your Grace, so you cannot possibly know how it would be for me, and Jocelyn, too. I will not have my child tainted if I can avoid it.''

"So you married an old man for protection rather than come to me.''

"What if I had?" she demanded. "Would you have offered to marry me, although I had no fortune or family to recommend me? There was no word of love between us.''

His gaze did not falter. "No, there was not, and I daresay you are right. I would not have married you. But I would have looked after you, for the child's sake.''

"So you say now.''

His brow lowered ominously and his eyes flashed with anger. "I tell you, I would have taken care of you and Jocelyn, even though—"

He fell silent.

"Even though I came to your bed uninvited like the worst sort of woman?" Verity finished for him.

"Yes."

"I had no way of knowing what you would do if I told you."

"So you gave me no chance to answer at all. That wasn't very honorable of you."

"Honorable? I had already dishonored myself— and the responsibility for what happened is mine, Your Grace. I came to you that night."

"I remember," he said quietly.

"Therefore," she continued after a moment, her voice strained, "I would not burden you with any of the resulting responsibility, either."

His gaze flicked away. "No doubt you thought that useless anyway."

"Perhaps. But all this happened ten years ago, and it is over with."

"It is not over with for me."

"We have to think of Jocelyn," she said, as much a reminder to herself as for him. "We have to consider what would be best for her. Surely you do not want everyone to know of her shame?"

"The circumstances of her birth are not *her* shame. I would have her know that she has a natural father, and that he did not abandon her, once he knew of her.

"She is my child, Verity," he continued firmly, "and I want to be a part of her life. I have not been part of a family since my mother died. I have relations, but that is not the same thing."

"I've explained—"

"Why did you do it, Verity?" he demanded, his even tones measured and deliberate. "Why did you come to my bed?"

"What does it matter now?"

"It matters to me."

Need burned in his eyes as he regarded her steadily, need and longing that was not a desire of the flesh, but something more.

In light of that longing, she could not keep this truth from him, either. "I was going to marry a man old enough to be my father in a month's time, and I wanted to know what it would be like to experience a young man's passion, just once," she answered, her whole body hot with humiliation.

"So I was the lucky candidate for assuaging your curiosity. Given that you burst into tears and fled from the room, I must assume I was a disappointment."

She shook her head. "No, you were not."

"Then I daresay I should be pleased that the experience was not without some merit."

"That *experience* gave me Jocelyn."

He crossed the distance between them, halting a few feet from her. "Why did you leave me that way?"

She backed away. "Is it not obvious? Because I was ashamed."

Mercifully, he didn't come any closer. "So you have been carrying this burden of guilt alone ever since."

"No, not alone. I told Daniel."

He stared at her incredulously. "You told your husband?"

"He was not yet my husband when I confessed what I had done, and the consequences. I was not that dishonorable."

"While I can commend you for your honesty in this instance, I must admit I am surprised he still married you."

"He loved me. He forgave me," she replied, "and when Jocelyn was born, he loved her as if she were his own child."

"He never cast your sin up to you?"

"No."

"The man sounds like a saint, too good to be true."

"He *was* a good man, and I gave him only base coin in return."

"Perhaps you shouldn't have married him, then."

"Yet I did," she retorted. "At the time, I would

have married him even if I had not been with child.''

"Because you spent an hour or two in my bed?''

"Because I loved him! Daniel saved me. He gave me a home when I had none. My father was a drunkard who had gambled every cent of his fortune, and he left me nothing when he died. If not for Daniel, I would have had to live in the streets, or throw myself on the mercy of the parish.''

"So Daniel Davis-Jones took in the poor orphan child and got a beautiful young wife in return.''

"You make it sound so sordid—but it wasn't like that. When I first came to live with him, he was kind and fatherly. I grew to love him very much. It was only later…much later…that he confessed his feelings for me had changed.''

"What of your feelings for him? Had they changed, too, from seeing him as a fatherly fellow to a lover? I think not, or I could not have tempted you.''

Her face reddened. "You would know *all* my shame, Your Grace? You would have me confess that every time he touched me intimately, I thought of you? That when he made love to me, it was your face I saw, your lips I kissed, your body I welcomed?''

"Is that true?''

"Yes!'' she hissed, tears starting in her eyes.

"Verity, did you never wonder what I felt that night?"

Taken aback, she stared at him with surprise. "I thought...I thought you would believe me to be an immoral woman," she stammered, "and you would have been right. I should never have gone to your room."

"I did not ask your opinion of what I *thought*. Did you ever give any consideration to how you made me *feel?*"

Her face flushed and she did not meet his gaze. "No," she admitted very, very quietly.

"You made me feel like a whore. You made me ashamed as I had never been shamed before."

She bowed her head as if bearing the weight of the world on her slender shoulders. "I apologized to Daniel, and now I apologize to you. I deeply regret what I did that night. I have regretted it every day since."

She lifted her face. "But I do not regret having Jocelyn."

He reached out to take her cold hands in his. "Verity, what you did that night saved me."

Her gaze anxiously searched his face, the faint light of hope dawning. "Saved you? From what?"

"From myself. From the road to ruin I was merrily marching upon. I needed to see the unthinking, unfeeling cad I was. I needed to have it made so clear, I couldn't deny it anymore. If you had not come into my bedchamber that night, by now I would be an even worse scoundrel than I was. You rescued me, Verity, and for that I will always be grateful.''

''You mean it,'' she murmured wonderingly.

He nodded and made a little smile. ''I confess I did not enjoy the learning of such a lesson, but I am a better man for it.''

He slowly moved his hands up her arms. ''I don't think a day has gone by that I haven't thought of you. And cursed you, at first,'' he confessed. ''But since my return, I have had my old self cast up to me a hundred times, and I can see the selfish beast I was.''

''I have thought about you, too, yet I only cursed myself.''

''You must promise me that you won't do that anymore.'' He inched closer. ''I needed to be saved, Verity, and you did it. I shall be forever in your debt, and glad to be so.''

Still cautiously, as if he were afraid she might shatter like glass in his arms, he drew her to him. ''Thank you, Verity, my beautiful savior,'' he murmured as he bent his head to kiss her.

This kiss was different from any they had shared: tentative, tender, as if they were both in the first flush of youth, and this their very first kiss.

Not wanting the feeling to end, Verity wound

her arms around his neck and gave herself up to the pleasure and yearning that filled her.

His tongue pressed gently against her lips and she parted them. With a low moan, she relaxed against him.

If only this *were* their first kiss. If only she had not given herself in marriage out of desperation and fear of poverty. If only she had not spent the past ten years in a cauldron of regret and dread that their secret would be discovered by her brother-in-law, and everybody else they knew.

Yet that was the choice she had made, the choice she had to live with, and it must still be so. The alternative was shame, ridicule, disgrace.

Reluctantly she pulled away, ignoring the look of loss in his eyes that mirrored what was in her own heart. "Please, don't kiss me again."

"No?"

"No. I am a respectable widow now."

"While I am still a lascivious scoundrel?"

"I...I am not sure what you are."

If he was disappointed by her answer, he gave no sign. Instead, he made a rueful smile and put his hand over his heart. "I am yours to command, Mrs. Davis-Jones. I promise I shall not do anything that will upset you." His smile disappeared, to be replaced by a blatant yearning. "If you will give me permission to visit Jocelyn. She is, after all, my child."

Verity tried to calm her fiercely beating heart, while her mind cried out that to allow him to come again would be folly, dangerous folly, that could end in disaster.

And yet…and yet he was Jocelyn's natural father.

She had denied him knowledge of his child for ten years and when he looked at her thus, with such hope and need, how could she refuse him? Perhaps if they were very careful…

"You may come to visit us Saturday morning. If the day is fine, we shall meet you in the wood, as if by accident."

He nodded and she relaxed a little, glad he would accept this. "Where are you staying?"

"With Myron Thorpe at his so-called hunting lodge."

"You know Sir Myron?"

"We were at school together. He tells me you and he barely know each other."

"He and I have nothing in common."

The duke's lips jerked upward in a small smile as he went to untie his horse. "Nor do I, except for our school days. I understand Jocelyn upset him over some cows?"

"That was an accident."

"So I thought." He paused, stroking his horse's head with his lean, strong fingers. "What if the day is not fine?"

Verity tore her gaze away from his hand. "You will have to wait until the next Saturday."

He nodded as he started to lead his horse toward the door. "Very well."

"I appreciate that you are willing to be careful."

"I gather I have little choice."

She could not deny that.

She hurried ahead of him to the door and peered out. "I don't see Jocelyn or Nancy through the window, so you can go back the way you came. What will you tell Sir Myron on Saturday?"

Galen untied his horse. "That I am going to the village."

"Why?"

"Why not?"

"You must have an excuse."

"In that case, I shall say I am going to the blacksmith's to have my horse's shoes checked. Myron will appreciate my concern over that, I'm sure."

"I hope you're right."

The duke led his horse to the door. She was about to open it for him when he put his hand over hers as it rested on the latch. At the sensation of the warm pressure of his strong fingers, she gave him a questioning, sidelong glance.

"Verity, I shall do my best to keep the truth about Jocelyn a secret, because you request it. You have the word of the Duke of Deighton, and while that may not have amounted to much ten years ago, it is different now. Because of you.''

For a moment she hoped—thought—he was going to kiss her again.

But he didn't. Instead, he shoved open the door and led his horse outside.

Verity didn't follow immediately. She couldn't. She had to regain control over her wayward emotions.

She pressed her fingers to her lips, the lips he had kissed so tenderly, robbing her of sense and reason and any notion of what was proper.

As she considered how his touch and his kisses stole her rationality, she wondered if she had just made another mistake that would be disastrous.

Chapter Six

"Are you expecting something to fall out of the sky?" Myron asked jovially, abruptly drawing Galen's attention from his contemplation of the weather.

Their greatcoats slapping damply against their Hessian boots, the stocks of their guns tucked under their arms and the long barrels pointing at the ground, they sauntered toward Myron's manor after a morning spent fowling. Behind them, gamekeepers carried the pheasants and grouse Myron had bagged, and the one bird Galen had killed.

"I was merely wondering if it was going to be sunny tomorrow, or wet."

Tomorrow he was to see Verity and Jocelyn, and the weather had to be fine. Otherwise, he would have to wait to see his daughter again, because of Verity's restrictions.

Once more he reconciled himself to the limits

she was placing upon his relationship with his daughter. It was, after all, understandable that she would wish to avoid scandal.

But at what cost? Her fears had already cost him ten years of knowing his child, his flesh and blood.

"It should be as fair as today," Myron said confidently, "if the sun is as red at sunset as it was yesterday."

"I hope you're right. I was planning on going into the village to have the blacksmith look at my stallion's shoes."

"You're going to Jefford to see the blacksmith, eh? Or the blacksmith's comely daughter?"

Galen bit back a peeved retort. Myron had been saying things like this the whole of his visit—not an insignificant price to pay for his accommodation. "I didn't even know the blacksmith had a daughter."

"He does."

"Believe me, Myron, I have no interest in the blacksmith's daughter, comely or otherwise."

Myron flushed with embarrassment. "I didn't mean to offend you."

Obviously he had not been as successful hiding his annoyance as he had thought. "No, forgive me for being peevish. I acquired a less than sterling reputation years ago quite of my own volition. Sadly, I fear it will follow me to my grave, no matter how I behave in my old age."

"Old age—oh, that's good!" Myron said with a chortle. "I don't think you need mourn your reputation. Some men would be only too happy to have your notoriety."

His tone made it rather clear that Myron was one such fellow.

"They might think so, until they did. I assure you, Myron, it is a hard thing to live down the follies and thoughtless acts of one's youth."

Myron nodded pensively, as if he were recalling a few follies and thoughtless acts of his own. Whatever they had been, Galen was sure they were minor at best, for Myron was too honest and good-natured a chap to do anything truly immoral.

Myron would have sent Verity scurrying from his room—or he would have scurried away, instead. Myron would have been a gentleman.

"I'm sure the ladies will be glad to hear of your reformation," Myron noted.

Although he remained silent, a hint of skepticism twisted Galen's lips. He was of a decidedly different opinion, for it wasn't only his valet who had expected him to resume his lascivious ways. Several married ladies he had sported with in his youth had already been shocked and angry when he had repelled their advances upon his return.

But he meant what he said to Verity: he was a changed man, and he would not debase himself anymore.

He would become the most respectable duke in the kingdom. He would do that not just for himself, but for Jocelyn's sake, because one day, when she was older, he hoped he could tell her the truth and on that day, he didn't want Jocelyn to be any more ashamed of him than she had to be because of his youthful misconduct.

On further consideration, becoming the most respectable duke in the kingdom would be too easy. All that meant was not wasting his money, or gambling or drinking to excess or having mistresses.

He must try to be as good and respectable as…as Verity's husband had been.

Damn Daniel Davis-Jones! How was he going to live up to a dead paragon?

"It must be something to have the women rush to you like hawks to the lure," Myron continued pensively.

"It must be something to be such an excellent shot," Galen replied, and it was no empty compliment. Myron had gotten his prey easily, always with one shot, and with a concentration that Galen had initially found astonishing.

He would never have believed that the voluble Myron Thorpe was capable of such silent determination and single-minded attention.

Myron beamed. "Practice, Your Grace, practice, that's all. Why, I shoot every day it's not positively raining."

"I wish I could say it was practice in my case, but unfortunately, it is only an accident of birth. If I were not a duke, I daresay my 'flock' would be considerably smaller.''

"Nonsense! You're a dashed good-looking fellow, too.''

"Another accident of birth. You cannot claim to have seen women flocking here. Why, except for your servants, we have been a couple of old bachelors this week.''

Myron smiled as if he were about to give Galen his heart's desire. "Ah, but not for much longer!''

They entered the back entrance of the manor, the sound of their boots echoing in the large stone foyer. Totally oblivious to the mud he tracked across the flagstones, Myron's eyes twinkled with pleasure as he sat on a wooden bench. "Can you guess what I'm getting at?''

"Let me try,'' Galen replied warily, subduing a sigh as he regarded his delighted friend and handed his gun to one of the many footmen who appeared in answer to Myron's booming voice, which seemed even louder in the cavernous entrance way. "You have female relatives about to descend upon your hunting lodge. If so, they must have made speedy preparations to get here so quickly.''

Giving his gun to another of the footmen, Myron chuckled. "Not *my* female relatives. I was too dashed clever to tell 'em, for a sillier lot I never met. Well, except for Charity, but she prefers her books anyway. Hates men.''

Galen did not pay much heed to Myron's description of the women of his family. "Are you telling me some of *my* relatives are coming here?''

"Exactly!'' Myron cried happily as he lifted up his foot so that yet another of the footmen could help him remove his muddy boots. "Lady Bodenham.''

Galen wanted to groan. "And George?''

"Gad, yes! Bringing his best hounds, too. I've been after him to lend me one for breeding forever.''

"I didn't know you knew him.''

"Met him at Newmarket one year. Bit mad for his dogs, of course, but that's understandable.''

Galen didn't think the often-neglected Eloise would agree, but the state of his cousin's marriage was less important to him than what Eloise's visit might mean. Surely she would want to see Verity, and perhaps Myron would invite her to his house.

"Your cousin also asked if she could bring her charming young friend, Lady Mary,'' Myron said with what was surely meant for a sly grin. "Naturally I said she was more than welcome. But I don't think she's coming out of any great desire to see *me*.''

Galen tried to look happy with this news. Indeed, he tried to *be* happy. He wanted a wife, he wanted a family, and he knew no reason he should not seriously consider Lady Mary. She seemed sweet and gentle, she was titled, she was rich and her father influential. "When are they arriving?"

"Impatient, eh, you dog? Tuesday afternoon."

Thank heaven it was not sooner.

"Stay back from the edge and try not to get wet," Verity admonished Jocelyn as her daughter set yet another twig afloat in the little stream that babbled through the wood. Overhead, the trees rustled and gray clouds moved swiftly with the brisk breeze. It was not yet raining, however, so she had decided to take Jocelyn to meet with the duke. She had not been precise about the time, though, and the air was chilly, so she hoped he would come soon.

She rubbed her gloved hands together. Try as she might to be calm and composed—and oh, how she had tried!—she might as well admit she could not be. She had never known a man who affected her as the duke did, even before she had met him in person.

She had thrilled to hear Eloise's whispered stories of his exploits. He had sounded like some sort of daring, handsome pirate-knight-Casanova all in one, a hero from tales of long ago who would not have been out of place at Arthur's Round Table.

When she had unexpectedly encountered him in

the flesh at Lord Langley's, she had been so thrilled she had hardly been able to speak. Then she had realized that compared to the self-confident, handsome Duke of Deighton, her future husband was ancient and as mild as a lamb.

So she had made her bad decision and gone to Galen.

To her surprise, when he sat up in his bed, so obviously naked, he had looked at her not with arrogant satisfaction, or lustful pleasure, but with a questioning vulnerability. If he had been arrogant or lustful then she might have fled at once. Instead, to see that doubt and wonder in his eyes, to see the query forming on his soft, full lips...

Silently he had touched and caressed and aroused with both tenderness and urgency, a potent combination she was helpless to resist.

No, not helpless.

She had eagerly given herself over to the pleasure he kindled. She had welcomed him into her willing body as if he were her lawful husband and that their wedding night.

Only afterward, when he had gently withdrawn, did she appreciate the full measure of what she had done.

She had given herself to a man not her husband, a man she hardly knew, as if she were a whore. Remorse—burning, agonizing remorse—had hit like a blow, and she had run away.

"I think somebody is going to have wet boots."

Verity jumped as if a snake had dropped down the neck of her pelisse and whirled around to see the duke coming toward her along the path.

He led his marvelous, impatiently prancing black stallion, and she didn't doubt it took an excellent rider to control such a beast.

"Pray forgive me," the duke said as he tied the horse's reins to a low branch. "I didn't mean to startle you."

"I was…thinking," she replied without meeting his direct gaze.

Jocelyn turned and her eyes widened with surprise before she ran toward him, then halted awkwardly a short distance from his mount. "Hello, Your Grace. What are you doing here?"

"This is a delightful surprise! I am visiting Sir Myron, a friend of mine."

His horse snorted, making Jocelyn jump. "Don't mind Harry. He sounds more fierce than he is. Are you fishing?"

"No!" Jocelyn cried, appalled. "That means touching worms!"

"Oh, dear," the duke replied gravely.

He glanced at Verity, who couldn't help smiling.

"I think I need to rest," he remarked, sitting on a convenient stump.

He didn't look like a man sitting on a stump, though. With his long dark hair, broad shoulders and regal bearing, he looked like a medieval monarch.

"Jocelyn likes to make boats out of twigs and leaves and set them sailing," Verity explained.

"I always get seasick when I go sailing, I am sorry to say," the duke confessed with a surprisingly sheepish grin.

Jocelyn stared at him, wide-eyed. "You've been to sea?"

"A few times. I much prefer to travel overland, if I can."

"The duke has been living in Italy."

"He told me when we were at Lady Bodenham's," Jocelyn said, grinning at her.

"Oh," Verity murmured, sliding him a glance and encountering that same merry, mischievous smile.

A warmth blossomed within her, made not of desire, but affection.

Or was her growing affection for the duke rooted only in a reflection of the deep love she had for her daughter, whom he had fathered?

"I fear I have gotten rather twisted around. Am I heading in the right direction for Sir Myron's?" he inquired.

Jocelyn giggled. "No. He lives back the other way." Then she frowned. "But I would be careful, Your Grace. He's always shooting things."

"Not people, I hope."

"No, not people," Jocelyn agreed. "But he might hit you by mistake."

"I look that much like a pheasant?"

Jocelyn giggled again and Verity smiled, too.

"No, you don't," Jocelyn said. "You're very handsome, though."

"Jocelyn!" Verity gasped.

The duke turned to her with feigned dismay. "You disagree?"

"Mama does think you're handsome, don't you, Mama?" Jocelyn demanded eagerly.

"I think the duke is not ill-favored, and I'm quite sure he knows that well enough without hearing it from me."

Jocelyn's eyes widened, and Verity wished she had not sounded so snappish—but really!

"I think your mother is very pretty, Jocelyn, nearly as pretty as you."

Jocelyn smiled and regarded her mother with pride.

"I must say Italy is considerably warmer than England at this time of year," the duke said as he pulled his supremely well fitting riding jacket a little tighter, and Verity was quite glad the flattery was apparently finished. "Jocelyn, if you sit on that log beside me, I shall tell you about the village where I live, if you would like."

Jocelyn nodded eagerly and did as he suggested.

The duke looked at Verity. "There is room for you, too."

She lifted the basket that she had slung over her arm. "I am going to pick mushrooms."

"Oh, good hunting, then."

He didn't look as if he minded at all that she wasn't listening, she thought as she strolled a little way down the path. Well, what else could she expect? He was here to be with Jocelyn, not her.

She went farther along the path, then looked back.

Jocelyn sat as if mesmerized, staring admiringly at the duke and listening attentively, while he smiled down at her as if...well, as if he loved her as a father should love his child.

She could believe that he did love her, just as she could believe his avowal that he was no longer the lascivious rogue of Eloise's tales.

Yet he was still exciting. Oh, yes, exciting and thrilling and altogether too tempting, perhaps even more so if he were as honorable now as he had been disreputable before.

Making a few more halfhearted attempts to find mushrooms, she wandered back toward them, drawn by his deep, fascinating voice, as well as her own curiosity about his life in Italy.

It sounded as if he lived very simply and quietly, with only a few close friends who visited from time to time. She wondered what he did to pass the days, for he was surely too vital a man to be content to sit in the sun.

Then he spoke of the villagers, sketching their characters in a few well-chosen words that easily allowed her to envision them, from Guido, his tempestuous neighbor with an equally tempestuous wife, to the absentminded local priest, Father Paolo.

He really was a wonderful storyteller, and if he were to confess that he had taken to writing books while he was abroad, she would have believed him.

"So, although my villa is quite small and plainly furnished, it is near enough to the village that when Guido quarrels with Angela, I can hear every word," he finished as Verity approached.

"Do they quarrel often?" Jocelyn asked.

"Nearly every day."

Jocelyn made a sour face. "How horrid."

The duke grinned. "They're not really angry and they make up every night. I hear that, too."

Verity stared at him, horrified by the implication.

"They sing opera when they've made up. Their favorite is *The Marriage of Figaro*. I would sing a little for you, but as I told your mother, I am no singer."

He paused and looked directly at Verity, his eyebrows rising questioningly. She flushed hotly, for she hadn't realized she was that close by.

"No luck finding any?" he queried.

"Any...?"

"Mushrooms."

"Oh, no. No luck."

"I saw some over there," Jocelyn said, pointing a little way through the trees to a shady clearing. She reached out to take the basket.

"I'll get them, Mama," she declared. She looked at her father. "I can *always* find mushrooms."

"She does have very sharp eyes," Verity confirmed.

"Then off you go and your mother can wait here with me."

Jocelyn took the empty basket and scampered off.

"Stay in the clearing," Verity called after her. "Don't go into the trees where I can't see you."

Jocelyn nodded her acquiescence and Verity turned back to the duke, who patted the log where Jocelyn had been sitting. "Won't you sit down?"

"I am content to stand."

"I don't sting, you know."

"I know."

"I won't kiss you again, either."

"Good." She decided she could sit beside him without repercussions. "Did you tell Sir Myron you were going to the blacksmith?"

"Yes." He looked at their daughter. "I assume

Jocelyn knows the difference between a mushroom and a toadstool.''

"Of course."

"We wouldn't want anybody to get sick."

There was something in his tone that made Verity give him a suspicious look. "No."

"Forgive me for upsetting you," he replied gravely. "I understand there was some...controversy...after your husband's sudden demise?"

He watched as Verity's chest rose and fell with a weary sigh. Given her reluctance to let him see Jocelyn, it might have been wiser not to mention this subject.

Before he could beg her pardon, she said, "The only people who had any suspicions about Daniel's death were his sister and brother-in-law. Nobody else."

"I am glad, and I regret raising such a painful subject."

"Tell me, Your Grace," Verity said after a moment's pause, "what do you do in Italy?"

"I read. I go to the taverna and indulge in arguments about politics. And I..."

"Entertain?"

He glanced at her sharply. "Not women."

"That isn't what I meant."

"I won't claim that I have been celibate these past ten years. My relationships have been mutually enjoyable, but not of long duration or serious intent, as the women knew at the outset.''

"That isn't any of my business, Your Grace."

"No," he agreed, "but I would have you know it, all the same.''

She didn't reply, and he wondered if he should have kept silent about that, too.

He didn't even know why he had told her.

Yes, he did. He wanted her to know he was free of any romantic entanglements. ''When I do not have any company, I write letters for people, and help young men bound for university with their English.''

"That does not sound like much for a man of your age and energy.''

"No, and I would do more," he replied, pleased, and yet not really certain if her words were a compliment or not. ''Unfortunately, for some reason, the men in the village don't like me chatting much with the women, so I find it best to stay near my property. And I do have matters of business to attend to, by correspondence.''

Verity didn't return his smile. ''Will you be going back soon?''

"That depends on what happens here." He cleared his throat and raised his voice as he nodded at Jocelyn. ''She looks as if her whole livelihood depended upon today's mushroom harvest, doesn't she?''

"She is very diligent, most of the time."

"Myron told me about the stampede."

To his delight, Verity made a wry smile. "Ah, yes, poor Sir Myron. He fell in a puddle trying to get out of the way."

"He didn't tell me that part."

"Perhaps it's too humiliating a memory."

He wondered if she meant anything else by that remark. "I have heard it said that you spoil Jocelyn."

Verity quickly turned an angry visage toward him. Before she could speak, he held up his hand to forestall her. "I was about to add that I don't agree. I have seen truly spoiled children, and she is not like them. You have done a marvelous job raising her, Verity. You should be very proud."

Verity relaxed somewhat. "I didn't raise her by myself, Galen. Daniel was as good a father as a child could wish for."

"I am grateful to him."

She gave him a sidelong glance. "I wasn't aware you had any contact with children."

"I was referring to my half brothers."

"Oh, yes, I heard some talk of them at your cousin's. The youngest sounds quite a rascal."

"Hellion would be more accurate. Hunt is the most spoiled one of all."

She cocked her head as she regarded him

thoughtfully. "I cannot say I have ever heard you described as spoiled."

"I don't think I was. Perhaps if I had been, I wouldn't have been so self-indulgent when I was allowed the freedom of youth."

"Why were your brothers spoiled and not you?"

"Half brothers," he automatically corrected. "For an explanation for that, you would have had to ask my father, and he is now deceased."

"I'm sorry. I didn't mean to upset you."

Wondering what she would make of the tension and dread that had been his daily lot in his childhood, Galen shrugged. "I should be able to react more calmly after all this time."

"The wounds of childhood run deep," she said softly. Sympathetically. As if she understood.

Compelled by her gentle tone, the sense that she could indeed comprehend, and suddenly weary to the bone of keeping his troubled childhood buried, the Duke of Deighton did something he had never done in his life.

He talked about his parents.

Chapter Seven

"I was never my father's favorite, even though I was the heir," Galen began matter-of-factly. "Perhaps if I had been more of a soldier or scholar...or perhaps if he hadn't married my stepmother."

"She didn't like you?"

"No, not at all. She had me sent away to school the first chance she had, and with my father's blessing, I'm sorry to say. She disliked me from the first moment she laid eyes on me when I was six years old."

"Why?" Verity asked softly.

"I fear I made a very bad impression."

"How can a child make a bad impression? You didn't hit her, did you?"

Galen smiled ruefully. "No, I didn't, but I wasn't exactly delighted by her arrival.

"I loved my mother very much. She was never

so cold and distant as my father. When I saw my stepmother and understood what my father had done, I was upset. Indeed, it was frightening to see this strange woman clinging to my father's arm like a leech. However, I tried not to cry. My father detested the sight of tears.''

"But surely she could understand," Verity protested.

"Apparently she did not, for she said, 'Why, what sulky little baby is this?' My father was very angry with me, and ...well, we never got on a better footing.''

"But you were only a child!''

"I was the heir, my dear," he replied, bitterness creeping into his voice, "and heirs don't sulk, or cry, or miss their mothers. Heirs keep a stiff upper lip at all times. Heirs do not have nightmares, or become homesick at school. Heirs do not hug or even touch their parents or their siblings or their servants, for any reason beyond the most necessary. They live without such base human contact.''

"Oh, Galen, I'm so sorry!''

His lips twisted into a sardonic smile. "I beg your pardon. An heir should not make excuses for himself.'' His gaze faltered. "Unfortunately, sometimes an heir is tempted to do so by a pair of sympathetic blue eyes.''

She reached out and took his hand. "I'm glad you told me, Galen," she whispered. "We both of us had a less than happy childhood. I never knew my mother. She died shortly after I was born. As for my father..."

"You spoke of him before. You need not open any wounds for me."

"You told me about your parents. Please let me tell you about mine. I would...I would like to."

He inclined his head in solemn acquiescence.

"I have already told you my father was a drunkard who gambled away the family fortune. Fortunately, I didn't see him often. I had a nurse when I was little, and then I, too, was sent away to school.

"However, in my case," she went on pensively, "I think that was for the best. School was a haven for me, especially after Eloise took me under her wing. It was also comforting to know what was expected of me, and how to behave."

She smiled a charming, wistful smile. "I wasn't always well behaved, unfortunately."

"Neither was I at Harrow, and I was infinitely worse after I left school."

"While I was very much better, until..."

"Until the night you spent with me."

"Yes."

He squeezed her hand, then reached out to caress her cool cheek. "Perhaps it is time we both forgave ourselves for that."

Still gazing into his eyes, she nodded. "Perhaps."

He reluctantly pulled his hand away and sought to lessen the tension between them. "I shall have to ask Eloise about your misbehaving when she comes to Myron's."

Verity's eyes widened. "She is coming to Sir Myron's?"

"He's quite delighted George is bringing his hounds. I shall likely smell of dog next time I see you. I really believe George would sleep with them if Eloise would let him." He frowned. "I won't come with her if she wants to visit you, so she will not see me with Jocelyn, if that is what's troubling you."

"I'm sorry, yet I truly believe we must be cautious. Eloise is a good and kind friend, but she does…"

"Gossip? Gad, I know it!"

Verity gave him a rueful grin. "Perhaps if she did not make her gossip so interesting, everyone would be less tempted to listen to her. She made you sound quite the romantic rogue, you know."

"The rogue may not have been much of an exaggeration," he confessed, "but as for romantic…no, I was far too selfish."

Her bright, intelligent, sympathetic blue eyes held his gaze. How wonderful it would be to have her near him always, to see that look and to know that here was one person who might understand him.

Who had been as lonely and love-starved as he.

"When are they coming?"

Torn from his reverie, he said, "Tuesday. They are also bringing Lady Mary."

Verity bent down and removed a bit of grass stuck to her boot. "Oh?"

"It is my fault, I fear. I told Eloise I wanted to get married, and it seems she has decided upon my bride for me."

Verity straightened. "And what do you think of the candidate?"

Although he knew he should not be, he was annoyed she sounded so matter-of-fact about it. "I suppose she might do."

"You don't sound very enthusiastic."

"Eloise is enthusiastic enough for both of us. She's quite convinced Lady Mary is the woman I should wed."

"Are you convinced?"

"There are worse women I could choose, I suppose."

"You do not love her."

Galen's heartbeat quickened. "No."

"You have not changed your opinion, then, from what you so eloquently expressed at Eloise's."

"Unfortunately, I think love in marriage is a

luxury the upper classes are denied. We must think of wealth and breeding before love.''

''And so you must take what you can get in the marriage mart.''

''Exactly,'' he replied ruefully. ''Forgive me for insulting you that night.''

''And you were very insulting.''

''I was angry with you then.''

Verity suddenly jumped to her feet. ''Jocelyn!'' she cried as she hurried into the clearing. ''Jocelyn!''

''What is it?'' he demanded, likewise getting rapidly to his feet and following her.

''I can't see her!''

''Jocelyn!'' he bellowed, a panic unlike anything he had ever felt throbbing through his body as he quickened his steps, passing Verity.

What if she had gone to the water and fallen in? Guido's nephew had drowned in a brook that was even shallower than this one.

''Here I am!''

Jocelyn peeked out from behind a large oak. He ran to her and scooped her up in his arms, as happy now as he had been worried before.

Jocelyn giggled as he spun her around. ''You've made me spill my mushrooms!''

''I'll help you pick them up.''

''Jocelyn, what did I tell you about going out of

my sight?'' Verity demanded. ''You frightened
me!''

''I wanted to see if I could find more and—''

''And what did I tell you about going beyond
the clearing?'' Verity repeated. Her voice was not
raised, but it was certainly firm, and her expression
stern.

As Galen bent down to retrieve the basket and
spilled fungi, he was ridiculously glad she wasn't
chastising him. He was also glad he was not the
one having to chastise Jocelyn.

''You said I wasn't to leave it,'' Jocelyn said in
a tremulous little voice.

''You understand that you frightened me?''

''Yes,'' Jocelyn replied with a sniffle.

Galen straightened. ''But she is safe and sound
and although some of the mushrooms may be
bruised, all is well,'' he said jovially, not wanting
his visit to end on a sour note, for it was growing
late.

Verity's smile was a little strained. ''Yes, all is
well, as long as Jocelyn understands that she is not
to disobey me like that.''

''I'm sorry, Mama.''

Verity's smile grew glorious. ''I know, little girl,
I know.''

''Mama!'' Jocelyn chided with a tone and look
eerily similar to her mother's only moments ago.
''The duke!''

Verity's face briefly twitched with the most comical remorseful frown Galen had ever seen. She turned to Galen and very gravely said, "I beg your pardon. She is not a little girl, Your Grace. Jocelyn is a *young lady.*"

"I was about to correct you on your error, for that is quite obvious to me," Galen replied with equal gravity, as if this were a debate of national importance in the House of Lords. "Now, regrettably, I must take my leave of you."

An expression flitted across Verity's face. Of regret?

He reached out and took Jocelyn's gloved hand. "Farewell, Miss Davis-Jones."

"Won't you come visit me again?"

"Perhaps if the duke is not otherwise engaged, he could visit us next Saturday," Verity suggested.

"And you'll stay for tea?"

Galen raised his eyebrows quizzically as he looked at Verity.

She hesitated for what seemed an eternity. "I think next Saturday, the duke may stay for tea."

It occurred to Galen that he could hardly be more pleased if he had been invited to dine with the Prince Regent.

No, that wasn't right.

He was infinitely more pleased to be invited for tea with Jocelyn and Verity.

"Oh, good, Mama!" Jocelyn cried, and he was delighted by her obvious enthusiasm.

"You start back, Jocelyn. I shall just say my goodbyes to the duke and be right along. Stay in sight, though," she warned.

Galen's heart sank. "Do you wish to rescind your invitation to tea next Saturday?" he asked quietly as Jocelyn started to skip through the clearing.

"Nancy helps clean the church once a month and next Saturday she will be there. I think it will be safe enough for you to come, if you travel through the wood, but I would like your assurance that you won't tell anyone where you are going."

"I won't."

"I shall also suggest to Jocelyn that you might be embarrassed if she tells Nancy, or anyone else, that she met you in the woods today because you had lost your way to Sir Myron's. I...I don't want to have to ask her to lie."

"Nor do I." He moved closer as if drawn by an irresistible force. He knew he should not kiss her again, and yet...

She gazed at him as if she, too, felt the same need, the same compulsion, the same irresistible desire.

"Mama?"

"I am coming, Jocelyn," Verity called as she turned on her heel and hurried away.

* * *

Tuesday morning Galen and Sir Myron went fishing, and Galen was glad to go. If Myron was quiet when he was hunting, he was even more quiet when the fish were biting.

Despite Galen's wish to be friends with Myron, the man's booming voice could get wearisome. It might have helped if Myron had had any interests other than hunting and fishing. Apparently he did not.

For once in his life, Galen was actually anticipating George's arrival with relish, for surely he and Myron would find much to speak of—to each other.

As before, gamekeepers dutifully followed their master and his guest as they walked back to the house, except today they carried the trout Myron had caught.

"Next time you will have better luck," Myron said sympathetically as he clapped a large hand on Galen's shoulder. "The trout might bite better after a rain."

"I fear I am no fisherman, Myron," Galen answered honestly as they neared the forcing garden, its many panes of glass glimmering in the sunlight.

"You fish for other things, eh?" his companion noted with a sly wink.

It was truly tiresome that Myron apparently could not realize that Galen was not the gay young blade out to seduce the entire female population of England. "I told you, Myron, I have given that up. I will be content to be the frog on the lily pad, waiting for an accommodating fly."

"Why, Your Grace! Sir Myron! Here you are!" Eloise cried, appearing from behind another glass building like some kind of genie.

She wore a turban like a genie, too, only with a drooping ostrich feather, and a spencer jacket that did not flatter her figure. "We arrived a short time ago and I said to George, 'If you insist upon going to the kennels right away, Mary and I shall take a turn around Sir Myron's garden until they get back.'"

"Have you developed an interest in the cultivation of pineapples?" Galen inquired gravely.

She pursed her lips before looking back over her shoulder. "I told you they would be coming this way," she said to somebody they couldn't yet see.

Nevertheless, Galen was sure he knew who it was—and he was right, for Lady Mary sidled timidly out from behind the pinery.

She was more conservatively attired for the autumn day in a hooded cloak of a becoming shade of sky blue trimmed with scarlet tassels. She looked very fresh and pretty, and very young and innocent.

She made him feel like an old reprobate, whereas with Verity, he felt...mature.

"Hello, Your Grace," she said with a shy smile.

"Sir Myron, allow me to introduce Lady Mary Seddens, the Earl of Pillsborough's daughter," Galen said, noting that Myron was blushing like a bashful youth.

Myron went to take Lady Mary's petite hand as she curtsied, then hesitated and awkwardly pulled it back. "I fear I smell of fish," he mumbled.

Lady Mary murmured that it was quite all right.

"So, you were prowling the grounds looking for us, cousin?" Galen said, turning the ladies' attention from the embarrassed Myron. "I must say it's a very pleasant coincidence that you came here the same time as I."

"Oh, Galen, really!" Eloise cried, her expression not nearly as scandalized as her tone. "It's a lovely day, that's all, and Lady Mary and I have been cooped up in the carriage since very early, so why should we not walk out and meet you? As for our visit, we should be the ones amazed, for you never visited Sir Myron before, or so I thought."

Galen realized he should have kept his mouth shut about the timing of their visit. "I agree I have been most remiss."

"I say, I've ordered my housekeeper to prepare a luncheon. I'm sure Mrs. Minnigan has it ready now." Myron smiled happily, then glanced at Lady Mary before turning to Eloise.

"I shall be delighted to walk in with you, and you don't smell of fish at all," Eloise said.

That left Galen to walk with Lady Mary.

Lady Mary looked after Eloise and her escort for a moment, then glanced up with bashful expectancy at Galen, who gallantly offered his arm.

"I really wasn't prowling about," she said quietly as she laid her hand upon his forearm, where it lay as limp as one of Myron's catch. "I have never seen a pinery before and was curious about it. If I had known you were likely to come this way…" Her voice trailed off into an embarrassed cough.

Again Galen reminded himself of his reason for returning to England. He wanted a wife and he wanted a family. This woman was young, she was rich, she was the daughter of an earl.

"You mean you would have purposefully avoided me?" Galen asked, letting his voice drop to a low, seductively intimate tenor. "I must confess I find that a distressing notion."

A flush spread upon Lady Mary's cheeks and her fingers tightened upon his arm.

Sadly, her touch didn't move him at all, and certainly didn't inspire him with any carnal longings.

He supposed he could try harder.

"Why, Sir Myron, you can't mean that!" Eloise suddenly exclaimed so loudly that even the gamekeepers started.

"What are you saying, Myron, that has so offended my cousin?" Galen charged with a hint of laughter.

After a very stern glance at Myron, Eloise turned back to Galen. "Sir Myron tells me he has never invited dear Mrs. Davis-Jones to his hunting lodge, and that he hasn't even seen her in months."

"Oh, your friend the widow? She lives nearby?" he asked disingenuously.

"I seem to recall mentioning it to you."

"Did you? Are you quite certain? Perhaps it was somebody else."

That wasn't exactly a lie, but judging by Eloise's furrowed brow, it was enough to make her doubt her memory.

"I don't think she would come even if I did," Myron muttered, looking decidedly uncomfortable. "We are acquainted, of course. I know what she looks like and something of her family."

Galen hurried to Myron's rescue. "Eloise, you told me Mrs. Davis-Jones doesn't accept invitations."

"But that doesn't mean he shouldn't ask her!" Eloise declared, apparently forgetting her own manners in her determination to set Myron's right.

"Well, now that I have company, of course I shall ask her. I shall give a dinner party and she will be invited," Myron replied manfully.

Galen's heart leaped at the thought of seeing

Verity another time. His arm must have moved, too, for Lady Mary suddenly gave him a surprised glance.

"A twitch," he whispered in a confidential aside. "I have an aversion to widows."

Lady Mary nodded. "I, as well," she admitted. "They make everything so gloomy and Mrs. Davis-Jones is so...so stern."

So Verity might seem if one did not know her well, Galen thought.

"She has not had an easy time of it," Eloise said with a hint of censure.

Galen silently applauded his cousin for coming to Verity's defense. He hated being unable to do it himself. Unfortunately, Verity's own determination to hide their relationship forced him to hold his tongue.

"I assure you, she was very different when she was young," Eloise continued. "She always had the most delightfully wicked ideas for getting back at our teachers at school. For instance, she was the one who came up with the idea of spreading molasses on the stairs as if it had spilled, then shouting 'fire' at the top of her lungs. Oh, dear me, the to-do as they all came scurrying down calling for us to get out and then stepping in it!"

While Eloise laughed at the memory, Galen imagined Verity as a child, her blue eyes sparkling with mischief, like Jocelyn's.

"She sounds like a terror to me," Lady Mary said. "I would never have done anything so horrible."

No, Galen silently agreed. He didn't think Lady Mary had it in her to come up with such a scheme. He didn't doubt that she had been a quiet, dutiful and dull child.

She would likely be a quiet, dutiful and dull wife.

"I shall be delighted to invite her," Myron said.

"Wonderful! I knew you were a gentleman," Eloise cried, "and I shall be delighted to take the invitation myself, as soon as you decide the day and time."

"Whenever you think best, Lady Bodenham," Myron offered. "I know nothing about dinner parties myself, so I shall count on your assistance—and Lady Mary's, too, of course," he finished, casting another timid glance at Galen's companion.

"Very well," Eloise answered, for she was never happier than when planning a party. "I shall insist that she come. I don't think it's good for a woman to waste away just because her husband is dead."

"Perhaps she prefers to be alone with her memories," Lady Mary suggested as they continued toward the house. "If a wife is very much in love with her husband, she may not want to socialize after he passes on."

She gave Galen another tentative smile, and he felt the noose tightening.

"Then she must be made to," Eloise declared. "It isn't healthy being cooped up all the time, and when I think how amusing Verity used to be...well, she mustn't be allowed to wallow in her grief."

"I must say, cousin, I had no idea you were an expert on grieving as well as child-rearing," Galen said, unable to keep silent, even if he did manage a tranquil tone distinctly at odds with his inner anger.

"Well, I'm not! And I might have known better than to talk to *you* about shutting oneself away," Eloise retorted, eyeing him pointedly.

"Eloise," Galen warned.

"Oh, very well, I shan't criticize you—but at least Verity had a reason for banishing herself from society. She didn't just take it into her head to do it on a whim."

Galen smiled, but only with his lips. "You know me so well, cousin. I lived ten years in Italy on a whim."

"Why *did* you leave England, then?"

As Lady Mary and Myron exchanged dismayed looks, Galen cursed himself for letting Eloise goad him. "As you said, on a whim. Then it seemed such an effort to return, only the death of my dear father could have persuaded me to do so."

"That reminds me of the time the duke put horse dung on the headmaster's door latch," Myron suddenly announced. "Then he hid all the candles on the poor fellow. The master came stumbling up the steps and put his hand on the latch and gave out the most horrified bellow I have heard. Sounded like a bull caught in a fence."

Lady Mary wrinkled her nose and Eloise frowned.

"Myron, you might have selected a more charming reminiscence," Galen said genially, thankful that his friend had tried to change the subject, even if he had selected this rather vulgar tale to tell. "I was very young," he said, by way of excuse to the ladies.

"You were fifteen!" Myron protested.

"Quite right," Galen agreed. "I was a young and immature fifteen, obviously."

"I shudder to think what you and Verity might have concocted had you known each other then," Eloise observed.

"Indeed, yes," Galen replied lightly as they walked up the terrace steps. "And if you think it worth the trouble, invite your dour, widowed friend. She didn't seem to enjoy the company when she was visiting you, Eloise, but of course this is a more small, select group," he said, implying that Verity was going to spoil the evening if Eloise did invite her and hopefully totally destroying any remaining inkling Eloise might have harbored that he had come to Myron's because of Verity. "Now if you ladies will excuse me, I have to wash and change."

"I, as well. Excuse me," Myron said with a bow.

"And I suppose I had better go see what George is doing," Eloise remarked with a long-suffering sigh as they departed.

Leaving Lady Mary slowly and pensively pacing on the terrace.

Chapter Eight

Saturday afternoon, Verity sat expectantly in her parlor, pretending to darn socks.

Well, she was not pretending, exactly. She really was trying to pay attention to the task at hand; unfortunately, her resultant stitches looked little better than Jocelyn's efforts.

She glanced at her daughter, whose feet were dangling and swinging as she sat on the sofa, reading—or reading as much as her mother was sewing, for she cast expectant glances at the window nearly as often as Verity.

Which meant, Verity told herself sternly, that she was acting no more mature than a ten-year-old.

And like her daughter, she had decided to wear one of her best dresses. It was black, of course, but cut a bit more fashionably than most of her mourning dresses, with tight-fitting long sleeves.

Jocelyn's dress was white, and Verity had allowed her to wear a pink ribbon in her hair. It had been over two years since Daniel's death, so a bit of color was not improper. Besides, Jocelyn had asked so sweetly, saying she wanted to look her best for the duke, Verity didn't have the heart to deny her.

Once again, she attempted to concentrate on darning.

"Mama, do you think you'll ever marry again?"

Verity started and jabbed herself with the needle.

"Whatever makes you ask that?" she asked as she made sure she wasn't bleeding.

"I was just wondering."

Verity turned her attention back to her work. "No, I don't think I shall."

"Why not?"

Again Verity looked at Jocelyn, this time with calm fortitude. "You loved Papa and you don't think anybody could replace him, do you?"

Jocelyn scratched her nose. "Not replace, Mama, of course," she said as if she had given this a great deal of thought. "But I know you've been lonely."

"I have you, and Nancy, and that's more than enough."

"The duke's awfully nice," Jocelyn said eagerly. "And he's handsome and I think he likes you a lot, and me, too. He's rich, besides. If he asked you to marry him, would you?''

''He will never ask me,'' Verity replied with an only slightly strained smile. ''I think he's planning on asking Lady Mary Seddens, a young and wealthy daughter of an earl.''

Jocelyn frowned darkly. ''Oh.''

''I want you to promise me you won't ask the duke any questions about such things when he comes, Jocelyn.''

''But—!''

''Jocelyn?''

''All right, I promise.''

''Good.''

Verity tried to thread a piece of yarn through her needle. It kept fraying, until she felt like screaming with frustration.

''You like him, though, don't you, Mama?''

''Who, dear?'' she asked as she wet the end of the yarn between her lips.

''The duke, of course.''

Verity was having so much trouble with the damnable yarn, she wondered if her eyesight was going. ''I like him.''

''If you were to marry again, wouldn't somebody like him be nice?''

Verity gave up and regarded her daughter. ''Yes, if I loved him.''

''If you married somebody like the duke, we

wouldn't have to be nice to Uncle Clive and Aunt
Fanny anymore.''

"We should always be nice to Uncle Clive and
Aunt Fanny,'' Verity replied as she put the un-
mended stocking away in the basket at her feet.
"They are our relations.''

Then they heard the sound they had been anticipating for the past hour: a horse coming down the
lane.

Jocelyn set aside her book and ran to the window. "It's him! It's the duke!''

Verity got to her feet. "Come away from the
window, Jocelyn.''

"But I want to watch—''

"Come away from the window. A lady should
try to moderate her excitement.''

Fine words she would do well to heed herself,
Verity inwardly commanded as Jocelyn grudgingly
obeyed.

"Let me look at you,'' she said as she surveyed
her daughter's attire and hair. "Have you washed
your hands and behind your ears?''

"Why would the duke look behind my ears?''

An excellent question. "I just want to be sure
you've done a good job. Let me retie your sash.''

"But Mama—!''

"It will only take a moment and the duke will
have to tie his horse. And remember what I said
about asking him questions.''

With obvious reluctance, Jocelyn submitted to her mother's ministrations.

When she was finished, Jocelyn whirled around, her blue eyes aglow. "Do you think he'll like the tarts?"

"I'm sure he will. You did a very good job."

A knock sounded on the front door.

"That's him!" Jocelyn cried. She started to run to the entryway.

"Jocelyn," Verity said, her throat suddenly dry as she followed her daughter at a more sedate pace. "A lady doesn't run."

If she were honest, she would add that she doubted she could have run to the door if she wanted to, for her knees felt shaky.

"Good afternoon!" Jocelyn said as she threw open the door and stood beaming at Galen Bromney.

"Good afternoon, Miss Davis-Jones. Good afternoon, Mrs. Davis-Jones," he said as he bowed.

"Please, won't you come in?" Verity replied stiffly, attempting to muster some calm.

As he came inside, she had the sudden sensation she was inviting a hurricane inside her house.

"This is a lovely home."

"Thank you. Won't you please come into the parlor, Your Grace?"

"I should be delighted."

Jocelyn skipped forward, while Verity maintained a dignified manner as she led the way, incredibly conscious that Galen was behind her.

She gestured toward the sofa in front of the windows.

His unremitting gaze fastened onto Daniel's portrait, which hung over the mantelpiece between two silver candlesticks.

"That's my papa," Jocelyn offered.

"He looks...nice," Galen said as he sat.

Verity took the chair opposite him.

"He was *very* nice," Jocelyn replied decisively. "Would you like to see my book?" she asked, picking it up.

Verity wished he would look anywhere but at her and the portrait as his gaze flicked between them.

"I should enjoy that very much, and you can tell me about it," Galen said. "Sit beside me here, and then I shall be able to see the pictures, too."

With a gleeful grin and not an inkling of shy hesitation, Jocelyn did as he suggested. She snuggled closer and Verity saw him tense. "Jocelyn, don't crowd the duke."

"It's quite all right," he replied with a hint of sharpness.

She instantly regretted making him think she would deny him this little coziness with his child.

Jocelyn opened her cherished book, the last gift

Daniel had given her before he died. "Let's read 'Ali Baba.'"

"Why don't you read it to me?" Galen suggested, turning his attention back to Jocelyn.

Jocelyn gave him another beaming smile, then started reading.

As she did, Verity didn't even make a pretense of sewing. Instead, she watched as Galen listened, his dark-haired head close beside Jocelyn's as he bent to see the pictures.

Verity had thought Galen Bromney would be out of his element when it came to conversing with children; however, as his behavior at Potterton Abbey and now in Jefford demonstrated, she was wrong.

He was wonderful with Jocelyn, and it was quite obvious she was happy being with him.

Was that so surprising? she asked herself. They were of the same blood, even if Jocelyn didn't know that. Perhaps there was a bond between them that neither ignorance nor distance could destroy.

If only she and Galen could begin again! If only she had not been so impetuous—but if she had not gone to him that night, she wouldn't have Jocelyn, and if it were not for Jocelyn, he would never have come back into her life.

Yet he could never be in their lives any more than this.

She stood up. "I shall make the tea. Would you

care for some tarts, Your Grace? Jocelyn made them.''

Galen gave his daughter a delighted smile. ''That would be wonderful. I'm sure they're very good.''

''They are,'' Jocelyn replied frankly. ''I spilled some jam, though, so Nancy was a little cross.''

''Nancy? Who is Nancy?'' the duke demanded, the underlying stern tone in his voice making Verity linger.

''Nancy is our servant.''

''What does she do when she's cross with you?''

''She makes me sit in the corner for a very long time.''

''Anything else?''

''If I have been very naughty, sometimes I don't get jam with my bread at dinnertime,'' Jocelyn complained, casting him a look that was both shy and indignant, as if appealing to his sense of justice and not sure he would concur.

His shoulders relaxed.

''I'm good most of the time,'' Jocelyn hastened to add, ''but sometimes I just *have* to do something and I don't think whether I'm behaving myself or not and then it's done and there's nothing I can do but say I'm sorry.''

''This sounds serious.''

Jocelyn regarded him quizzically. ''Don't you

ever do things that other people might say are naughty? Don't you ever feel you just *have* to do it, or you'll burst?''

''I must confess I am guilty of hasty acts without proper consideration,'' Galen said honestly, giving Verity a glance that set her heart racing. ''What naughty things have you done?''

Jocelyn frowned and shook her head. ''I'm not telling!''

''Not treason or some great crime, I hope?''

''No!''

''You are not a highwayman, perchance?''

''No.''

''Do you break into houses or pick pockets?''

''No,'' she said with a giggle.

Galen heaved a sigh of relief. ''I am very glad to know I am not in the company of a career criminal,'' he remarked gravely. ''And I think you really like Nancy, even when she's cross.''

''I *love* her!'' Jocelyn declared emphatically.

Galen told himself he had no right to be jealous. Jocelyn hadn't even met him until a month ago; she had likely known this Nancy all her life.

''Although it is rude to leave our guest alone, I could use Jocelyn's help with the tea things,'' Verity said.

''I offer my humble assistance,'' Galen said, rising. ''I do know how to boil water and I would much rather go with you to the kitchen.''

"Very well," she replied with a smile, the sort of smile that belonged to a girl who could play pranks on her schoolmistress. "I would like to see a duke in a kitchen."

Galen made an elegant bow in response. "I shall endeavor not to disgrace myself if you will but show me the way."

"Follow me, Your Grace."

"Gladly," he murmured as he obeyed.

"May we use the good plates?" Jocelyn asked as she skipped ahead of them down the hall.

"For a duke, we would use nothing else."

"Does she always dance like that?" Galen asked quietly.

Verity tried not to notice how close beside her Galen was. "When she is happy, she does. Apparently you have that effect on her."

"I am glad to think she doesn't find me imposing."

"There may come a day you wish she did," she replied ruefully. "She can be quite stubborn."

"So can I."

He put his hand lightly on Verity's arm to delay her, his supple fingers wrapping around her forearm. "I truly didn't mind her sitting so close."

"You tensed," Verity replied, wanting him to understand why she had chided Jocelyn.

"It's true that I am not used to such easy familiarity." He gave her a sardonic, yet woeful, smile. "The only intimacy I have known in the past thirty years is the sort we have shared."

The intimacy she so well remembered. "I am sorry to hear that."

"I was sorry to live it."

Their gazes met and held for the briefest of moments—yet in that instant, Verity felt as if the world had suddenly tilted on its axis.

Or love—sweet, delicious, devoted love—had slipped unnoticed past the barriers of years and experience and gained a foothold on her heart.

His hand dropped from her arm and she stepped back, actually unbalanced.

"Mama, what's taking you so long?" Jocelyn called from the kitchen.

Feeling as if she had been startled awake, Verity hurried to the kitchen, a large, whitewashed room fitted with all that was new and modern, and where Nancy usually held sway with despotic authority.

Then she gasped at the sight that met her eyes.

Jocelyn stood precariously on a stool in front of the tall dresser, reaching up for a covered plate on the top shelf.

"Jocelyn!" Verity cried, hurrying around the large pine worktable to grab her by the waist. "What are you doing?"

"The raspberry tarts are up there."

"You should have waited. I will get them when

it's time to serve them," Verity said as she set her daughter on the stone floor.

"I only wanted to get them down for the duke," Jocelyn mumbled, her head lowered.

"You might have fallen," Galen said sternly, coming to stand beside Verity.

When Jocelyn's bottom lip started to tremble, Galen went down on one knee. "If you had fallen, you might have hurt yourself, and I would have been very upset, especially if you injured yourself trying to get a treat for me."

He rose and reached for the covered pewter plate. "And what if these had fallen, too, and been squashed? A tragedy!"

That made Jocelyn smile, while Verity suddenly remembered why they were in the kitchen and went to fill the kettle.

"Stop!"

Verity halted in midstep at Galen's command.

Then he winked at Jocelyn, destroying the tension that had momentarily filled the room, before he strode forward.

"Madam, if you please," he said imperiously. "I am to boil the water, am I not?"

"Yes," she agreed.

He took the kettle from her, their hands momentarily touching.

Galen cleared his throat. "Yes, well, as I said, I

can boil water," he remarked. "Sadly, that is all I can do."

"If you can boil water, you must be able to boil an egg," Jocelyn noted.

"Alas, I have never been taught, and when I think of all the times I have craved a boiled egg and been without a servant..." He sighed mournfully, yet his eyes twinkled as he set the kettle on the range.

"I can boil an egg," Jocelyn said proudly.

"Is it difficult?"

Verity stifled a smile while she got out the tea and the pot and the other accoutrements for their refreshment.

"Not at all! Mama, can we do an egg for the duke?"

"Yes, certainly," Verity replied. "Fetch one from the pantry and I shall get a pot."

Jocelyn hurried from the room while Verity headed for the row of newly tinned pots to find one suitable for a single boiled egg. She glanced over her shoulder at Galen, who was studying the range and adjoining oven. "These look very modern," he remarked.

"Daniel wanted the best."

"I would say he got it."

Verity lifted down a suitable pot and faced him. "Nevertheless, we must seem rather rustic to you."

"On the contrary, I envy you."

"You envy me?"

He nodded slowly. "I envy you your charming house, and your simple life. I envy you your friends, for even Eloise stands up for you, and there are not many for whom she would do that." He came around the table toward her. "Most of all, I envy you all the time you've had with Jocelyn."

She flushed hotly and her grip on the pan tightened. She could almost feel his lips upon hers again, and the strength of his powerful arms embracing her. "Galen, I—"

"I've brought the biggest one I could find!" Jocelyn crowed from the doorway.

"What do we do now?" Galen asked, going to Jocelyn and deftly sidestepping a large basket of potatoes near the leg of the table.

"Well, first we get the pot."

"I get the pot," Galen said. He took the one Verity proffered without looking at her and she was, naturally, grateful for being spared another awkward moment.

"Then you fill it with enough water from the bucket near the range to cover the egg."

"Enough water to cover the egg," Galen repeated as seriously as if these were the instructions for a medical procedure. He took the pot to Jocelyn, who still held the egg.

"Now I put in the egg, and we put it on the range. We let the water come to a boil, and then when it has done that a little while, we *plunge* it into the cold water in the bucket," she finished triumphantly.

"I see," Galen said, doing as he had been told with regards to putting the pot on to heat. "So now we must wait for all this water to boil."

"And while we do that, Jocelyn and I will set out the tarts and tea things on a tray to take to the parlor."

"Oh, surely we can have our tea here," Galen asked with a hint of wistfulness. "I'm tired of formality."

"But you're a duke!" Jocelyn protested.

"That may be, but I have never had the pleasure of having tea in the kitchen."

"But I don't think—"

"Jocelyn, the duke is our guest, and what did I tell you about when we have guests?"

"Oh."

Galen had no idea what precise instructions Verity had given Jocelyn about the treatment of guests, but he suspected it was along the lines of accommodating oneself to their wishes—and for that, he was glad. He meant what he said: he had never had the pleasure of tea in a kitchen.

He very much liked this kitchen, too, with its air of comfort and domesticity. He liked the range and the oven; he liked the dresser with its knicks and scratches that told of daily use; he liked the smells of the smoked ham and onions hanging from the rafters. He liked the potted flowers on the sill.

Most of all, however, he enjoyed the company, even if he was also more disconcerted than he had been for years.

He had told himself he could return to England because, surely by now, his reputation would be nearly forgotten, replaced in popular gossip by the fresher scandals of the past ten years. Instead, he had discovered that the moment he appeared, everything he had ever done seemed to leap, rejuvenated, into people's minds.

That he might have learned to live with.

He had also convinced himself that *he* had forgotten things over the passage of ten years. He had believed he had forgotten how he had felt when Verity had come to his bedroom, that he no longer remembered the texture of her skin, the softness of her lips, or the way her breast felt in his palm. He told himself he could not recall the low murmur of need she had made in the back of her throat when he had first kissed her, or the heated passion that had coursed through his body when she removed her nightdress.

Surely he had forgotten how her blue eyes could flash with desire, or how her shy smile seemed to reach deep inside of his soul to something long buried, and bring it to shattering, vibrant life.

What a fool!

And he wished he had never seen the portrait of Daniel Davis-Jones. He had envisioned the older man as either frail and elderly, or old and fat.

It was very disturbing to see that Daniel Davis-Jones had been what women would call a "fine figure of a man," with friendly dark eyes beneath iron-gray brows. The fellow had had broad shoulders, no extraneous plumpness and masculine hands.

Hands that had also touched Verity. Intimately.

Chapter Nine

Galen rose abruptly.

"I thought I should check on the water," he said by way of explanation to his startled companions. "I don't want to be remiss my first time boiling an egg."

Jocelyn and Verity exchanged smiles, and another shaft of painful regret lodged in his heart. What would he not give for this to be his home? he thought as he went to the range. His wife. His child, who knew he was her father.

His eyes clouded as he peered into the pot. *Get a hold of yourself, Galen,* he silently commanded. *Gentlemen don't cry.*

"Is it boiling?" Jocelyn asked as she left the plate of tarts, surreptitiously licking a bit of jam from her finger.

"Not yet, but the kettle is about to, I think. Do

you mind if I open the window?'' he asked Verity.
"I'm finding it rather warm."

"So am I," she murmured, not meeting his
gaze.

"The kettle's boiling, Mama!" Jocelyn cried,
and Verity moved as if glad of the distraction.

"So is the water for the egg," she observed.

"Ah!" Galen hurried toward the range. "I am
to take it off—"

"Wait!" Verity cried as Galen went to grab the
pot handle with his bare hand. "You'll burn yourself."

"Good God, how stupid of me," Galen muttered as Verity, holding a cloth, went to take the
pot herself.

"No, please just give me the cloth," he said to
her. "I would like to do this all myself, if you
don't mind. Otherwise, I shall feel utterly incom-
petent and as if all that remains for me is the life
of a totally useless aristocrat."

Verity handed him the cloth. "I don't think it
would be possible for you to be useless."

"Why not?" he asked as he wrapped the cloth
tightly around his hand. "I have not been terribly
useful thus far in my life."

"But you're a duke!" Jocelyn exclaimed from
the vicinity of the tarts.

"And you're a little girl who's going to be in

trouble if you've been sticking your fingers in that tart again,'' Verity observed pointedly.

"I haven't!''

"Little Jack Horner...'' Galen murmured as he glanced at Verity with a twinkle in his eye.

"I haven't!'' Jocelyn protested.

"We believe you, don't we, Your Grace?''

"Of course we do,'' he replied, unable to resist the compulsion to add a slight emphasis on the delightful "we'' even if he was not at all pleased to be addressed by his formal title.

"However, Jocelyn, I must point out that I have done nothing to earn the title except be my father's eldest son,'' he continued as he carefully lifted the pot from the range and set it on the hob. "Two of my half brothers have already accomplished more than I, and they are quite a bit younger. Now what do I do?''

"Take that big wooden spoon and lift out the egg, then put it in the bucket very carefully,'' Jocelyn ordered.

Galen nodded, then bit his lip as he gingerly followed her orders. When the egg was successfully deposited in the bucket, he looked at his young teacher. "Is that all?''

"That's all! Well, except for taking it out and removing the shell, of course.''

"Oh, yes, of course,'' Galen said as he lifted

out the egg and put it on a waiting plate before sitting down on the bench beside it.

Verity and Jocelyn had set the table with delicate porcelain plates, cups and saucers, white napkins and silver teaspoons.

"The tea is ready now," Verity said, sitting opposite him and beside Jocelyn, who was directly behind the plate of tarts, one of which showed definite signs of tampering.

Verity picked up a cup and saucer. "Tea, Your Grace?" she inquired in as formal a tone as if they were in Buckingham Palace, or as if she were a duchess.

A duchess.

"Indeed," he replied just as gravely.

"Do you take sugar?"

"No, thank you."

"Milk?"

"No. I prefer my beverages unembellished." He glanced at Jocelyn. "Plain," he whispered out of the side of his mouth, which made her giggle.

As Verity handed him his tea, she gave Jocelyn a pointed look, then the plate of tarts. "Would you care for a tart, Your Grace?" the little girl asked.

"I should be delighted. They look lovely," he said sincerely, reaching toward the plate and selecting the tart beside the one that looked as if a little finger had been conducting exploratory surgery.

"Nancy helped me, but I did most of the work," Jocelyn said proudly as Galen took a bite.

The Duke of Deighton had eaten many a toothsome morsel in England and abroad, but he thought he had never tasted anything as good as little Jocelyn's tart, and he told her so in no uncertain terms.

As she flushed with pleasure, he realized Verity was looking a little put out. He regarded her quizzically, while Jocelyn bit into her tart with great appetite.

"Jocelyn, when you have finished your tart, you may fetch more milk from the pantry and I'll let you have a little tea," Verity said.

Jocelyn's rather jammy mouth widened, then she fixed Galen with a curious stare. "You have brothers?" she demanded.

"Not with your mouth full," her mother said softly, quite unlike the sort of correction Galen's father had often visited upon him.

"I have three half brothers," he said, reaching out for another tart. "Buckingham, Warwick and Huntington. Buckingham is in the navy, Warwick is in the army and Huntington is still at school."

"Those are funny names," Jocelyn said as she wiped her mouth on a napkin.

"Unusual," Verity corrected softly, and again Galen was struck by her gentle method of correcting their daughter's mistakes.

"Yes, they are," he answered. "My stepmother chose them because we are related to the families."

"I would like to have a brother or a sister," Jocelyn said wistfully.

"Perhaps someday you will."

"How can I, when my Papa is dead—unless Mama gets married again."

"Get the milk, please, Jocelyn," Verity said as a very becoming blush spread over her cheeks.

Verity continued to blush as Jocelyn left the room.

"I didn't mean to remind her of her loss," Galen said, all the while wondering what Jocelyn would think if he offered to marry her mother.

She didn't seem to find the idea of her mother's remarriage unconscionable, and he felt distinct pleasure at that realization.

Then he noticed Verity wasn't blushing anymore. She was regarding him with a censorious expression. "You shouldn't patronize her."

"When have I been patronizing?"

"When you told her her tarts were the best pastry you had ever tasted."

"It's quite true," he protested.

She gave him a skeptical look.

It had been a long time since anyone had looked at the Duke of Deighton like that, without deference or awe—and he liked it. They might be any husband and wife sharing a simple domestic disagreement.

He thought of Guido and Angela, and had a sudden urge to burst into song.

"I like simply made foods better than fancy ones," he said instead, "and I'm sure Jocelyn took as much care with them as the baker who made the Prince Regent's wedding cake. Besides, I think those tarts had a special ingredient sadly lacking in the things I am served."

"What might that be?"

"Love."

"Oh." Verity couldn't meet his steadfast gaze; fortunately, before the silence could get even more awkward, Jocelyn came back bearing a pitcher of milk.

Verity poured a copious amount of milk into a cup, then added a little bit of tea.

Jocelyn settled herself back on her chair, looking quite pleased with the state of things. "Is your brother the captain of a ship?"

"No. My half brother is a lieutenant. The last I heard, Buck had taken ill and was recuperating at Gibraltar."

"I trust it is nothing serious," Verity said.

A coldness crept into the duke's voice. "I assume he's doing well. I have not heard otherwise. I would have been informed if he was dead."

"Oh," Jocelyn gasped, obviously taken aback by the unfeeling nature of the duke's last words.

So was Verity.

He immediately appeared contrite; nevertheless, there was a look in his eyes that confirmed his relationship with his half brothers was not a close one.

"Is your other brother an officer, too?" Jocelyn asked warily before she took another sip of her beverage.

"He is an adjutant to the Duke of Wellington."

"Really?" Jocelyn breathed, obviously impressed. "Was he at Waterloo?"

"Yes. So you see I am in earnest when I say they have all done more than I.

"Well, not Huntington, perhaps," he corrected with a smile, "but he is well on his way to distinguishing himself at Harrow for the quality of his pranks."

He fixed his gaze onto Verity. "I understand your mother also had a reputation for that sort of thing."

"You did?" Jocelyn asked, staring at her mother with awe.

"I suppose Lady Bodenham told you some of my…activities?" Verity asked warily.

"She did, indeed. I particularly liked the one with the molasses."

At that reminder, Verity couldn't help smiling.

She had been punished by having to stay in her room every evening for a month, but it had been worth it to see Miss Mintley's face when she stepped in the sweet, sticky substance.

"What about molasses?" Jocelyn asked with avid curiosity.

"Oh, no," Verity demurred, shaking her head and smothering her smile. "I'm not confessing to anything or giving certain little girls any ideas, especially ones who have no trouble coming up with mischief on their own."

"Then what Sir Myron Thorpe told me is true?" Galen asked with astonishment in his voice and a twinkle in his eyes. "Can it be true that this young lady who has such a promising future as a pastry chef did indeed cause a cattle stampede down the main street of Jefford?"

Jocelyn giggled. "No," she managed to say as she set her cup down with a rattle.

"The gate was unlocked and the cattle got out on their own," Verity explained.

Then, to Galen's delight, that mischievous gleam again lit her blue eyes. She looked at her daughter as if they were fellow conspirators. "Unfortunately, she also decided to practice her Indian war cry."

"Her Indian what?"

"My Indian war cry. Like this."

Suddenly Jocelyn threw back her head and emitted the most bloodcurdling yell Galen had ever heard.

"No wonder the cattle stampeded," he said when she stopped and looked at him proudly. "I nearly ran out of here myself."

He gave Verity a wry smile. "I daresay it's a good thing you live so out of the way, or your neighbors would all have apoplexy." He looked back at Jocelyn. "Wherever did you learn to do that?"

"My friend's uncle is a sea captain who's been to America. He taught her, and she taught me."

"Sometimes it sounds as if we've got a war in our garden," Verity said.

"We *have* to scream like that when we play Indians."

"As long as you don't try burning anybody at the stake again," Verity cautioned.

Galen's eyes widened. "I beg your pardon?"

"It was only one time," Jocelyn assured him. "And we didn't really set the wood on fire. But we pretend that's what we're doing on Guy Fawkes Day, and we do our war cries then. It's great fun."

"Since I was never allowed to make much noise as a child, I shall have to take your word for it."

"You couldn't make any noise?" Jocelyn asked, dumbfounded. "However did you do it?"

"I don't think I played the same sort of games."

"Would you care for more tea?" Verity inquired, thinking it best to leave the subject of Galen's childhood.

"Indeed, I would enjoy it, and another tart, if I may."

"Of course," she replied.

He smiled again, slowly, the corners of his mouth lifting ever so slightly while his eyes...

"Your face is all red, Mama."

"Is it?" she asked, putting her palms over her cheeks. "It must be the heat of the range."

"I do think it's exceptionally...warm...in this room," Galen noted in a low, somewhat husky voice.

Did he feel as she did at that moment, as if there were some kind of cord of desire stretched between them that was constantly tightening whenever they were together?

The kitchen door suddenly flew open as if a great gust of wind had hit it.

But it was another force of nature: Nancy, who spoke without looking in the vicinity of table as she shut the door.

"Sweet simmering stew, what is this world coming to?" she exclaimed, more flushed and flustered than normal, even given her usual unrelenting brisk pace. "Here I was thinking how glad I was we've seen the last of them Blackstones for a while, when who do I meet but that Achilles' Heel Rhodes, or whatever the dumpling of a man calls himself!''

Verity quickly got to her feet, fighting the urge to order Galen from her house or Jocelyn to her room, so that Nancy wouldn't see the resemblance and guess the truth.

It was not that she didn't trust Nancy. She did. But she also knew better than to trust to Nancy's ability to keep a secret. Nancy often spoke before thinking. She might let the truth slip out.

''I believe you mean Claudius Caesar,'' the duke said calmly as he, too, got to his feet.

Nancy whirled around and stared. ''Who the devil are you?''

''Nancy!'' Verity cried, aghast at her language, while Jocelyn clapped her hand over her mouth to stifle a giggle.

''This is the Duke of Deighton,'' Verity continued, accepting what she couldn't change and doing her best to act as if nothing at all were unusual about this situation.

''The master of—what was it you called him?'' Galen inquired evenly, ''a dumpling?''

Nancy went so red Verity was afraid she was having an attack. ''Your Grace, this is Nancy Knickernell, my servant—and my friend.''

Nancy's considerable self-esteem reasserted itself. ''Forgive me for speaking out o' turn, Your Grace,'' she said without a particle of contrition in her tone, "but he spoke most impertinently to me."

"I am sorry to hear it and I apologize for him," the duke said in his most conciliatory tones.

Galen's deep voice and hazel eyes could be most conciliatory.

Indeed, Verity watched in amazement as Nancy's expression actually softened before her very eyes. Under normal circumstances, Nancy could stay angry for days. She was always out of sorts for the whole duration of one of Clive and Fanny's visits.

"The duke stopped by to visit," Verity said.

Then Jocelyn went to stand beside him and Verity felt a shiver of dread as they smiled at each other.

Given their dark curls and the slope of their chins, Nancy would surely see the similarity.

All Verity could hope was that since Nancy was ignorant of her rendezvous with the Duke of Deighton at Lord Langley's, she would put any likeness down to coincidence.

Yet what would she make of the duke's easy familiarity and presence in the kitchen?

They should have rendezvoused in the wood again, by "accident."

"We met him at Lady Bodenham's, you see," Jocelyn clarified.

"So your mother told me," Nancy replied without a hint that she noted anything untoward about the pair.

Verity dared to breathe a little easier.

"As delightful as it is to meet you, Nancy," the duke said, "I fear I have overstayed my welcome and must be on my way. Perhaps Miss Jocelyn will see me to the door?"

"Do you have to go?" Jocelyn asked mournfully.

"Alas, I must."

"You'll come back for another visit, won't you?" Jocelyn asked.

"The duke may not have time. He is visiting here, you know, and Sir Myron—"

"Can easily spare me, I'm sure. I would love to come back and visit you, on one condition."

"What's that?"

"You will make some more tarts."

Jocelyn grinned and nodded rapidly.

"I took the liberty of putting Harry in your little carriage house," he said. "My horse," he added for Nancy's benefit as he went to the back door. He put his hand on the latch, then turned back. "Oh, by the way, I believe Lady Bodenham is likely to call this afternoon."

"Oh?" Verity murmured.

"With an invitation to join us for dinner at Sir Myron's later this week, if I am not mistaken. I do hope you'll be able to come."

"I shall have to th—"

"We can go, can't we, Mama?" Jocelyn pleaded.

"I fear this will be an invitation only for your Mama, this time," he said gently. "It will be too late in the evening for you."

Jocelyn frowned.

"But I am hoping you and your friend will allow me to play Indians with you at least once while I am in Jefford. I'm sure I can manage a war cry."

Then the Duke of Deighton let loose a loud screech that made Nancy stare as if he had suddenly gone mad, while Verity and Jocelyn's mouths gaped with astonishment.

"Forgive me, Nancy," Galen said with a bow. "I was practicing my war whoop. I didn't mean to startle you. Until later, Miss Davis-Jones, Mrs. Davis-Jones."

His gaze held Verity's for a moment before he opened the door.

And then he was gone.

"Sweet simmering stew!" Nancy muttered. "You had a duke in the house and you gave him tea in the kitchen."

Verity and Jocelyn turned toward her. "He said he wanted to have his tea here," Verity explained.

"Why? To see how the poor folk do?"

"He said he'd never had tea in a kitchen before," Jocelyn replied.

Nancy sniffed. "I can believe it." She looked a little mollified as she put on her apron. "Well, who are you to say no to a duke when he asks something, eh?"

"I saw no harm in it," Verity replied.

"I think the duke is very nice looking, don't you?" Jocelyn demanded "He's got the nicest smile—but he does need to have his hair cut."

"No doubt he's just being careful," Nancy replied sarcastically as she wiped the crumbs from the table. "I wouldn't let that Magnus Pompous near my head with anything sharp for love nor money."

"He's fun, too," Jocelyn continued. "He played football with me at Lady Bodenham's. He wasn't very good at it, but he was very nice."

"Who boiled the egg?"

"The duke did," Jocelyn said, grinning.

"Never!"

"He did," Verity confirmed. "He said he had never cooked an egg, so Jocelyn showed him. And he was very impressed with the tarts."

"He said they were the best he had ever had!"

Not for Nancy a doubt of the duke's sincerity when it came to praise of her baking. She fairly beamed. "Well, then I hope he does come back—only next time, he shall have some pie." She grew serious. "Now out of my kitchen, the pair of you, or they'll be no dinner. I've got to set things to right.''

Content to let Nancy rule her culinary kingdom and anxious to avoid any further discussion of the duke, Verity obeyed.

Later that afternoon, Verity sat in her bedroom, thinking about Galen and Jocelyn and herself, and the visits they had shared.

Unfortunately, once the pleasure of his company and the euphoria of realizing that Nancy apparently saw nothing amiss wore off, she had come to the conclusion that they could not continue to see each other.

It was simply too much of a risk. While it seemed Nancy didn't notice any resemblance this time, she might start to wonder if Galen became a frequent visitor. Nancy also knew that Verity had gone to school with the duke's cousin, so she might make assumptions of previous meetings.

No, despite how much it was going to disappoint Jocelyn, she couldn't risk having Galen come to the house again. She would have to explain to her daughter that nobles had many calls upon their time, and she hoped Jocelyn wouldn't be upset for long.

She would also have to hope that since Galen was a mature man with more knowledge of the cruelties the world could inflict upon the innocent, he would understand and agree with her.

As for how she felt about this decision…her feelings didn't matter. Jocelyn's future happiness was much more important.

"There's a man in a purple coat knocking on our door, Mama!" Jocelyn called from the parlor.

While Nancy answered it, Verity went to her bedroom window and looked outside.

Galen had predicted aright. Eloise had come and was seated in a barouche as if part of a parade in London. Even more noticeably, she wore an orange bonnet trimmed with yellow plumes that was surely considered the height of fashion and a long pelisse of the brightest yellow Verity had ever seen.

Between the brim of the bonnet and the color of her cloak, Eloise looked like a giant canary.

Glad that she had been forewarned and prepared, Verity hurried down the stairs and reached the bottom just as Eloise entered. Whatever Nancy had made of the footman, she was openly and unabashedly staring at Lady Bodenham.

Up close, Eloise's garments were even more remarkable, especially when one considered how many hours must have been spent applying the orange and green ribbons, making the looped buttonholes and stitching the tucks and gathers.

Whatever Verity thought of Eloise's outfit, however, it was very clear from Eloise's satisfied smile that she thought she looked very well indeed.

"Why, my dear, I had no idea your house was so charming and quaint!" Eloise exclaimed as she sighted Verity. She fluttered toward her like a distracted moth as she surveyed the papered hall. "But so utterly out of the way! I was sure the driver had taken the wrong way when he turned into your lane."

Verity thought it was a wonder she hadn't heard Eloise's exclamations. "What a pleasant surprise, Eloise. You may close the door now, Nancy, and take Lady Bodenham's pelisse."

Eloise removed her yellow cloak to reveal a gown of a more subdued yellow, yet equally betrimmed with green and orange ribbons. She handed her pelisse to Nancy, then her bonnet and kid gloves.

"And I'll make some tea, will I?" Nancy queried as if she weren't quite sure of what one was to do with such a visitor.

"That would be wonderful. Thank you. This way, Eloise," Verity said quickly, steering Eloise toward the parlor before Nancy mentioned Galen's visit that morning. "Whatever brings you to Jefford?"

"I'm visiting that charming fellow, Sir Myron Thorpe. George met him at Newmarket and they got to talking about dogs…well, what else would George talk about?'' Eloise noted with a sigh. ''At any rate, dear Sir Myron invited us to visit, and I thought, why not? I shall be able to see my dear friend Verity again, too. So, here I am!''

''I am so glad you did,'' Verity murmured. ''Won't you please sit down?''

Eloise perched on the sofa. ''I will confess my coming here was not simply to visit Sir Myron.''

''No?''

''No. My cousin, the Duke of Deighton, came first and when I heard that, it did occur to me to wonder if he had come in pursuit of you, the rogue, so I immediately got George to write. Myron naturally reiterated his invitation, and here we are.''

''You were worried about your cousin's possible pursuit of me?''

''You're still very pretty, you know, Verity. Fortunately, Galen hardly remembers you from your visit to our home, except as a dour widow, which just goes to show he can't have paid much heed to you at all,'' she finished triumphantly.

''I'm glad of that,'' Verity said with genuine relief, although not for the reason Eloise would no doubt ascribe.

Galen had obviously and successfully misled Eloise about his reason for coming to Jefford, and thrown off her suspicions.

Eloise suddenly waggled her long index finger at her friend. ''Now I must insist you confess. You've been keeping secrets from me, you naughty thing!''

Chapter Ten

Verity's hand instinctively went to her throat as if to strangle a moan of dismay. "Secrets?"

"I had no notion that your house was so large and au courant," Eloise said with a playfully angry expression. "I confess I had visions of you in a thatched cottage—a nice one, to be sure, but considerably smaller and less up-to-date than this delightful house."

Verity couldn't quite subdue a sigh of relief. "Thank you. We're very comfortable here."

"I daresay you are, and I understand a little better why you are so loath to leave it—although I'll say again I don't think you should keep to yourself so much."

"I take it Sir Myron is very interested in hunting dogs, too," Verity said, changing the subject. "Did you bring any of your dogs?"

"George brought his dogs." She smiled beatifically. "*I* brought Lady Mary."

The woman Eloise thought Galen should marry.

The woman she should want Galen to wed, Verity told herself, a young, pretty, sweet woman from a titled and wealthy family with not a hint of scandal attached to her. "Oh?"

Eloise inched forward excitedly, then looked around as if expecting spies lurking nearby. "My cousin, the duke, told me himself he's looking for a wife, and Lady Mary will be *perfect* for him!"

She waggled her finger at Verity again. "Oh, I know what you're thinking—what woman in her right mind would marry a cad like that? But I do believe Galen has changed his ways. Why, he's been in England over a month now and there's been not a word of any liaison between him and a woman, of any kind. No angry husbands marching about London denouncing him for a scoundrel, no actresses pretending to kill themselves over him, no fathers claiming he's defiled their daughters."

Verity smiled. "How disappointing."

Eloise's eyes shone with amusement. "You know very well I am not the only person who found his former life fascinating! I well remember you hanging on every word about the latest scandal when I told you about them."

"I was much younger then."

"Oh!"

Verity wished she had held her tongue, especially since Eloise was right. "I am only saying that I would not find such a man fascinating now that I know better. A cad may be exciting for a little while, yet I suspect he leaves behind far more sorrow than happiness."

"You are likely right," Eloise agreed. "And then some of those women! I assure you, my dear Verity, I don't know where he found them! I think he must have gone looking for the worst possible mistresses he could find."

She leaned forward again. "I don't think he cared a fig for any of them, either, although he was more than generous. He only wanted to upset his father. The former duke was quite a martinet and very stern with Galen, always. I don't recall ever hearing the late duke say anything to Galen that wasn't a reprimand. He was not nearly so hard on his second wife's children."

So it was as Galen had said, and worse. Her heart went out to the boy who, while lacking for nothing material, must have longed for a kind and loving word.

Was it any wonder he would find affection when he could?

"Galen's certainly been more serious since his return," Eloise continued. "And he's been the perfect gentleman with Lady Mary. I don't think he's even touched her, except to escort her in to dinner."

Did Galen's touch affect Lady Mary as it did her? If so, Verity wouldn't find it difficult to discover that Lady Mary was hoping with all her heart to become the Duchess of Deighton.

In her case, such a thing was not impossible.

But Verity would not be jealous. She could not be. She had no right to be.

As Nancy entered with the tea things and set them on the small table beside Verity, Eloise suddenly noticed the portrait over the mantel. "Good God! Is that your late husband?"

"Yes, that's Daniel."

"My dear, I had no idea!" Eloise peered at the portrait. "He was a very good-looking fellow, I must say!"

"Yes, he was. The silver candlesticks were a wedding gift from his weavers. They all liked him, too, so you know he was more than nice looking. He was truly a kind man and excellent employer. I was very fortunate."

Her task completed, Nancy straightened and looked directly at Eloise. "He was the best man and master you'd ever be likely to meet!"

"Oh, yes, certainly," Eloise stammered, clearly unused to servants expressing themselves so forcefully.

"You may leave everything, Nancy."

"Yes, Mrs. Davis-Jones," Nancy replied with great formality.

Apparently quite satisfied with the reaction she had elicited from Eloise, Nancy triumphantly marched out of the room.

"She has been with my husband and his family a long time," Verity offered as both excuse and explanation as she poured the tea.

"Oh, yes, I see. And what business was your late husband in again? Cotton, wasn't it?"

"Daniel was a wool merchant. He had started to do some business in cotton, too, but he sold his interest in the mills to his brother-in-law before we were married."

Eloise's eyes widened. "With all the money to be made in cotton these days, he sold his interest? Why, mills are veritable gold mines."

"When he saw the deplorable conditions there, and when he couldn't convince the men who bought his raw cotton to amend them, he stopped dealing in cotton altogether rather than be part of it."

"Oh!" Eloise emitted, taken aback. "That seems rather extreme."

"I thought that you would understand better than most why I would not wish to be involved in such an exploitive system, Eloise," Verity said softly, "and why I would not be married to someone who was."

A look of understanding dawned on Eloise's face. "Oh, yes, yes, certainly," she murmured. "I had forgotten."

Eloise sighed as she eyed one of the jam tarts and laid her napkin across her knee. "Still, it is the way of the future, I suppose."

"I fear that, as well, so I give what money I can spare to those who are working to change it."

She realized Eloise wasn't really listening and subdued another sigh. Eloise inevitably found serious discussion boring. "Would you care to have a tart?"

"They look excellent," Eloise said as she took one. She bit into it daintily, then regarded Verity with a pleased smile as she wiped her fingers. "Now, I have the most delightful thing to tell you! Sir Myron wishes me to extend an invitation to dine with him, and his guests, this Wednesday."

Verity's first impulse was to refuse. She didn't want to see Galen with the woman who might become his wife.

But then practicality intruded. The dinner party would surely provide an opportunity to arrange a meeting with Galen, so she could tell him that he could not visit them again.

She would not tell him that at the party, of course. First, she dared not speak to him in private for more than a moment, and second, she didn't doubt that he would be visibly upset when he understood what she was asking.

Or perhaps it would be better if she waited...

"You need have no qualms about getting there. Sir Myron has told me he will be happy to send his carriage for you," Eloise wheedled. "You simply *must* come! I'm afraid I've given poor Sir Myron a tongue-lashing about not inviting you sooner, and if you don't, he'll be miserable."

Verity could well believe that Eloise had thoroughly chastised her hapless neighbor. "I wouldn't want Sir Myron to be miserable."

"Wonderful! And you need not fear any impropriety on Galen's part, either. Lady Mary will be there, and George, too, of course."

"Please tell Sir Myron it is very kind of him to invite me and I shall be pleased to accept."

"Oh, sweet sufferin' savior!" Nancy muttered the morning of the day Verity was to dine at Sir Myron's.

"What is it?" Verity asked, looking up from the sock she was redarning to see Nancy glaring out the parlor window.

"They're back," Nancy said, turning toward her mistress with an expression of complete disgust. "At least this time the miser hired a curricle from the inn."

That tone and that look could only mean one

thing: Clive and Fanny had come for another visit.
But why so soon and why today, of all days? If
Clive and Fanny were visiting, it was even more
important to tell Galen to stay away, yet she could
hardly attend a dinner party when she had guests
of her own.

"First that Julius Caesar valet, then the duke,
then that woman, and now *them.* Who's next, the
Duke of Wellington? Admiral Nelson?" Nancy demanded, her hands on her broad hips as if she truly
expected Verity to answer. "I don't know what
I'm going to do for more food. I can hardly get
them to notice me at the butcher's now that Sir
Myron's got company. His cook ordered enough
for a militia regiment. It's the same at the fish market, too. I swear you'd think nobody ever visited
Sir Myron before."

"Make up the guest room, please, Nancy. I shall
answer the door."

"Gladly, if it means I don't have to say hello to
them two too soon," Nancy said as she stomped
out of the room.

Verity sighed as she took off her apron and
smoothed her hair. She would have to write a note
expressing her regrets to Sir Myron. It was unfor-
tunate she couldn't write to Galen, too, but that
was absolutely impossible.

Clive's familiar rap sounded on the front door
and she hurried to answer it.

"So, this time you are home," he declared jovially as he sauntered inside, a valise in his hand and Fanny creeping in behind him like his unworthy servant.

Verity's lips tightened. Upstairs, she could hear Nancy punching the pillows with rather extreme vehemence.

Verity wished she could punch a few pillows herself.

"You look out of sorts, dear sister," Clive observed with a hint of offense, as if anything less than obvious pleasure at seeing him was an insult. "I hope you are not ill?"

"No, merely tired," she replied.

As Clive removed his hat and held it limply in his hand, his lips pulled back from his teeth in a broader—and unattractive—smile. "Where's Nancy?"

"Upstairs. Here, I shall take that for you," Verity said, reaching out for his beaver hat.

After a deferential glance at Clive, Fanny took off her dove-gray cloak and likewise handed it to Verity. Clive strolled into the parlor without waiting for an invitation, and Fanny shuffled in behind him. With a frown, Verity laid their garments on the small chair she kept in the hall for Jocelyn to use when she put on her boots.

"I am happy to hear you are not ill," Clive said when she joined them. "Sir Myron would be most upset if you were unable to attend his dinner party tonight.''

"How do you know about his dinner party, or that I was invited?" she asked, trying not to sound suspicious.

"We met Sir Myron in the village," he explained. "He was kind enough to extend an invitation to us."

Verity wanted to groan with despair. As disappointing as it was to miss the party and an opportunity to arrange a private meeting with Galen, the prospect of attending with Clive and Fanny was infinitely worse.

She was tempted to plead an indisposition, but that probably wouldn't stop Clive from going.

Better, surely, to go with them.

"He mentioned you were already invited, even though you should still be in mourning. Of course, these are degenerate times."

"Degenerate times," Fanny ventured to echo.

"I thought him too important a neighbor to risk offending," Verity replied.

"Quite right. No matter what should have been done, Sir Myron expects you to be there now, so of course we shall all go." He gave his wife a censorious look. "Sit down, Fanny!"

Fanny obeyed, swiftly sitting on the sofa. Clive strolled over to stand in front the hearth, his hands behind his back as he rocked slightly on his toes.

"What brings you back to Jefford so soon?" Verity inquired.

"I wanted to tell you personally how well the mills have been doing, and to allow you another opportunity to invest."

"I cannot afford it."

To her surprise, Clive's mouth didn't get that pinched look it usually did when she gave him that excuse, something she had been doing ever since Daniel passed away. "Oh, well, it will be your loss, not mine."

His genial response only created new suspicions, and his next remark confirmed them. "I shall ask Sir Myron and his guests if they would like to make a fine return on a small initial investment."

Whatever happened tonight, Verity knew, it was not going to be a pleasant evening.

As he tried to make a proper knot in his pristine white cravat, Galen could not recall feeling more anxious before a dinner party. He had experienced varieties of anticipation, certainly. In his youth he had known an excited thrill when there would be a woman he was hoping to seduce in attendance. He had felt amused anticipation sometimes, when the company promised to be ridiculous. Upon his return to England, however, he had only looked forward to being bored by the empty conversation of people about whom he did not, and could not, care.

Except for Verity's last night at Potterton Abbey. He had anticipated meeting her there with a host of mixed emotions: excitement, curiosity, anger and frustration.

Now he wondered what Verity was feeling. Since she had accepted the invitation, she must be more confident that people wouldn't suspect anything regarding Jocelyn's parentage, and that pleased him. He hated to think of her worried. She should be happy and carefree, as she deserved to be after all she had been through, especially having to endure her in-laws. One good look at Clive Blackstone during a single conversation at the village inn where he and Myron had stopped for a drink on the way home from a day's fishing, and he thought he had a fair idea of the measure of the man.

Toady was the best word to describe him, for the fellow had nearly fallen over bowing when they met. Then he had been so obsequious, he quite outdid anybody else Galen had ever met, and Galen had been dealing with obsequious people all his life.

The wife was, unfortunately, of a type Galen had encountered once or twice before, a wife so totally dependent and devoted to her husband, it seemed as if she could hardly breathe for herself, let alone think. Fanny Blackstone had watched her husband as if he were the center of the universe, while he had to be reminded to introduce her.

Indeed, Blackstone treated his wife as dismissively as some men would their horse or their dog, and Galen didn't doubt he thought himself superior by nature to any woman, even Verity.

He hated to think how difficult it must be for Verity to have this man in her life.

There was also the need to keep their secret to make him nervous. He would do all in his power to prevent anyone from suspecting he and Verity had met years ago.

More difficult than that, though, was going to be masking his feelings for Verity. He would have to hide his affection that had blossomed into something he now felt in the depths of his heart, and disguise his desire.

How did Verity feel about *him?*

He suspected that she liked him, and he knew there was a powerful physical attraction—yet he did not know if there was more on her part, as there was on his.

He had to find out.

Tonight, somehow, some way, and with all the subtlety he could command, he would find the means to speak to her privately.

Not to try to ascertain her feelings with any certainty, but only to arrange a meeting. A secret rendezvous. Then he would try to discover—

"Do you require some assistance, Your Grace?" Rhodes inquired.

Galen had forgotten Rhodes was there. "Yes, please. I cannot seem to get the damnable thing tied."

Despite his offer to help, Rhodes approached as if being led to the guillotine.

"Whatever is the matter, Rhodes? You look like you're going to your death."

"I was just thinking, Your Grace," Rhodes intoned gravely as Galen lifted his chin and Rhodes took hold of the ends of his cravat.

"It seems they would be thoughts of a serious nature."

"They would be, yes."

"Not too troubling, I hope?"

"I've found out your little secret."

Galen's throat constricted and he coughed.

"That's a bit tight," he said as an excuse. "What secret might that be?"

"I was wondering why we've come to Sir Myron's, but now it's as plain as the buttons on a peacoat."

"I came because Myron was my friend at Harrow. I have been very remiss not accepting his invitation before this."

"If you say so, Your Grace, but it's quite a coincidence Sir Myron happens to live in the same village as that pretty widow,'' Rhodes noted before he stepped back to examine his handiwork.

"I don't chase after widows, Rhodes.''

"I thought you might be making an exception,'' his valet replied as he went to fetch Galen's evening coat. "She's very pretty.''

"I did not come because of Mrs. Davis-Jones,'' he replied, which wasn't exactly a lie. He had originally set out for Jefford to see Jocelyn again.

He drew on his coat. "My answer hasn't made you any happier,'' he noted.

"If you're not here after the widow, are you after Lady Mary?''

"I should rather think the question is, is Lady Mary after me? She followed us here, after all, Rhodes, not vice versa.''

Rhodes did not smile. "I would merely like to know the state of things with regards to my future, Your Grace. If there's going to be a wife, I would like some time to prepare myself, and to do all I can to stay on her good side.''

"If I am going to be married, Rhodes, you shall be the first to know. Will that suit you?''

Rhodes relaxed visibly. "Yes, Your Grace, it will.''

"Just to satisfy my own curiosity, what do you think of Lady Mary?''

Rhodes began to brush Galen's coat vigorously.

"Pretty. Sweet. Good-natured, or so I hear. Fine qualities in a wife, I think. There you are, Your Grace. All finished."

Galen checked his reflection in the long mirror in the corner of the bedroom.

What did he want in a wife? He wanted a woman like Verity—loving, gentle, passionate, intelligent, as well as an excellent mother and wonderful lover.

Hell, he wanted Verity. He needed her.

He loved her.

Chapter Eleven

As Galen left his bedchamber and headed toward the wide stone stairs, he could already hear Myron's booming voice in the drawing room.

At the bottom of the stairway, he paused a moment to straighten his shoulders and prepare to be charming to Lady Mary, while paying as little attention to Verity as possible, until he could speak to her alone.

It would be enough to be in the same room with her.

No, that was a lie. However, if he was denied the banquet, he would have to accept what crumbs he could.

"So then I knew I had the beast for good!" Myron declared as Galen strode into the drawing room decorated with pictures of Myron's deceased relatives and horses and hounds.

Attired in a pretty and youthful gown of pink satin and with her hair done in a modern yet simple style, Lady Mary regarded Myron with what looked like awe, making the poor fellow blush as red as an army tunic.

With a start, Myron turned away from the admiring Lady Mary. "Oh, Galen, here you are!"

"And he landed the trout," Galen finished, for he didn't doubt Myron was relaying his version of that day's fishing. "I would have lost it for certain. Ladies, I must say our host is the finest man with a line I have yet encountered."

This was quite true. Galen had only been fishing one other time, in his distant youth, and had hated it so much, he had never cared to repeat the experience until now.

"I told you Galen wouldn't keep us waiting long, Mary," Eloise said playfully.

Ensconced on the sofa, Eloise wore a gown of blue muslin printed with something that Galen supposed were intended to be birds. Instead, they looked like splotches of spilled wine. Her hair was again tortured into a fashionable bundle of braids, curls and ringlets, and adorned with ribbon.

Galen sauntered toward Lady Mary. As loath as he was to deceive her, he had to avert any suspicion as to where his affection really lay.

There was also the extremely unwelcome notion

that if Verity did not reciprocate his love and refused his offer of marriage, he might have to settle for someone else. "I am flattered you were impatient for me to arrive."

When Lady Mary returned his smile, he realized that if he asked her right now to be his wife, she would probably agree. Would she be eager to accept if she knew she would be his second choice?

He turned toward Eloise. "Where's George?"

"His favorite dog has a cold in her chest and he wanted to stay with her," Eloise answered. "He assures me he will be joining us for dinner—after he has washed and changed, of course."

Her peeved expression made Galen suspect that there had been an argument over this, yet he didn't dare hazard a guess as to who the winner had been, George for staying with his dog until the last possible moment, or Eloise for getting George to come to dinner at all.

"Mr. and Mrs. Blackstone, Mrs. Davis-Jones," a footman intoned from the door.

Clive Blackstone bustled into the room as if shoved by a supernatural force and headed straight toward Galen instead of his host.

His nondescript wife came trailing behind, and after her came Verity, wearing a stark black gown unembellished by any ornament, her hair in the plainest of knots at her neck—and yet she would not be any more beautiful to him if she wore a queen's raiment. Her cornflower-blue eyes shone brightly and her cheeks glowed with vitality.

For the briefest of instants, she caught his gaze and held it.

That moment was not nearly long enough.

"Your Grace, how wonderful to see you again!" Blackstone cried as if they were old friends who had not seen each other in years.

"Quite," Galen answered.

He glanced at Lady Mary, who couldn't have looked more horrified if Clive Blackstone had been the Minotaur. She sidled away from the newcomers toward a somewhat dumbfounded Myron.

Meanwhile, Eloise ignored the Blackstones and went directly to Verity.

"Mr. Blackstone, Mrs. Blackstone, allow me to introduce you to Lady Mary Seddens, the Earl of Pillsborough's daughter," Galen said, leading them toward the lady and their host. "Lady Mary, Mr. and Mrs. Blackstone."

"So pleased to make your acquaintance, Lady Mary," Clive breathed in seeming ecstasy.

His wife murmured softly, "So pleased."

Lady Mary held out a limp hand, which Blackstone immediately snatched up as if she had money in it to give him. Lady Mary just as quickly snatched it back.

Meanwhile, Galen wondered what Eloise and Verity were talking about. Short of walking over to them, however, he had no way of discovering their subject because, unfortunately, he had no reason to intrude, other than to listen to Verity's voice.

A footman came to the door and summoned Eloise, leaving Verity momentarily alone.

Was this his chance already?

Then Eloise turned to address them.

"It seems dinner is served, and my husband will not be joining us after all," she declared with obvious annoyance. "His dog is not any better."

She marched toward Galen. "I fear, cousin, I am going to have to commandeer you to take me in— or perhaps Sir Myron will?" She raised her brows and glared at him.

"Oh, yes, of course, glad to," Myron stammered.

"And I shall escort Lady Mary," Galen said, fighting the urge to suggest that Verity go in to dinner with him.

"I shall be delighted to take my sister-in-law," Blackstone offered.

Galen didn't like the way the man smiled when he said that, while his wife bowed her head with such submissiveness, Galen could believe she possessed no backbone, either figuratively or in reality.

His jaw clenched. She could very well be the type of woman who would forgive her husband anything, including lusting after another.

"No, no, it's quite all right," Verity said, her vivacity a direct contrast to Fanny Blackstone's lack of it.

And so it was decided. Eloise took Myron's arm, Galen escorted Lady Mary, then came the Blackstones and finally Verity, all alone.

As the meal progressed through an astonishing number of courses and several glasses of wine, Verity wished she had stayed at home. It now seemed certain that Galen was courting Lady Mary, and she was more than inclined to accept him.

Verity reminded herself that she couldn't complain about that. She and Galen could never be together, so she should be glad to think of him married to another and making a happy life for himself. She could not fault him for wanting a wife and other children.

Nor could she fault Lady Mary for desiring him. How could she, when even now she yearned to be with him herself?

But, oh, she didn't want to have to watch him

woo his future wife, or to watch Lady Mary make it plain that she was anxious to take on that role.

Being there with Clive and Fanny only added to her torment. Clive kept up a running stream of chatter complimenting Sir Myron on his house, his servants, the meal, until Verity wanted to order him to be quiet. Meanwhile, Eloise spoke continually to the unresponsive Fanny about her family connections.

Verity's heart nearly stopped when she caught the name "Lord Langley," but in another moment, Eloise had moved on to another subject.

That reference was too close for comfort, nonetheless. What else might Eloise inadvertently say? What might Galen say that could fuel speculation, especially with Clive in attendance?

She should have stayed at home! She should have found another opportunity to speak with Galen.

As if she did not have enough anxiety, Lady Mary innocently inquired about Clive's business.

"Cotton mills, Lady Mary," Clive eagerly replied, his face lighting up as if he had just been awarded a prize.

No doubt he felt he had, for he had been given the opportunity he had undoubtedly been waiting for. "Wool previously, cotton now. As I'm constantly telling my dear sister-in-law, mills are the place to invest and there could not be a better time than the present.''

''Mrs. Davis-Jones and I were speaking of this very thing the other day when I had tea at her charming house,'' Eloise declared.

''Why, you said nothing to me of this,'' Clive chided.

''I did not think you would care to hear about my conversation with a friend.''

''That fellow in our class at school—the one with the six sisters—didn't his father have money in mills?'' Myron asked Galen.

''Thompkins?'' Galen replied as if barely interested. ''Is that where the family fortune came from?''

''That, or spices,'' Myron said, his brow furrowing with concentration.

''I would not be at all surprised to learn it had been cotton,'' Clive declared. ''A small investment now will surely yield great dividends.''

''I confess I don't understand investments,'' Lady Mary murmured, looking at Galen with a shy smile.

''You have no need,'' he replied pleasantly.

Sir Myron stroked his chin meditatively. ''Investments can be devilishly hard to fathom.''

''I shall be happy to explain it to you,'' Clive offered. ''It's really very simple.''

Verity recognized the greedy gleam in Clive's eyes. She wouldn't be surprised if Clive managed to persuade Sir Myron to invest a considerable sum before the evening was over.

She fastened her gaze on Sir Myron. "You invest your money and he builds a mill which then employs poor men, women and even little children to work slavish hours for very small wages."

Clive's face reddened with annoyance, but Verity continued nonetheless. "Have you ever been in a mill, Sir Myron?"

His bovine eyes widened. "No, never...no."

"The conditions for the workers are horrendous," she continued, paying no heed to Fanny's pale, timid face or Lady Mary's furrowed brow, or Eloise's frown. "They are herded in those huge buildings like animals, working long days in the heat without a moment's pause."

"Verity!" Clive warned.

But he had no right to silence her.

Galen made a wry little smile. Of approval? She couldn't wonder about him now. It was more important that Sir Myron understand there was more to investing with Clive than a potential profit. "I didn't raise the subject, but if Sir Myron is thinking of investing in your business, he should understand *all* that it entails."

"She would have factory owners house their

workers in palaces and feed them on ambrosia,'' Clive said through clenched teeth.

"I would have your workers paid a decent wage, and I would be ashamed to be a part of any business that forces children as young as Jocelyn to work all day and into the night in heat and noise, with no fresh air."

"You speak your mind very decidedly," Lady Mary observed with quiet astonishment.

"Especially for someone whose family made their money in the slave trade," Clive snapped.

Verity felt, rather than saw, Galen's gaze on her as the heat of shame filled her.

"What my dear sister-in-law fails to appreciate is that we do pay wages, and if we are to do that, we must make a profit. Nor are our workers slaves. They are free to leave our employ at any time. There are plenty of others willing to take their places, which would not be so if the conditions are as horrendous as my kindhearted sister-in-law implies."

"Mr. Blackstone makes an excellent point," Sir Myron mused aloud. "Nobody's forcing them to stay, after all."

"Nobody is offering them any alternative, either," Verity countered.

Feeling in need an ally, she instinctively fastened her earnest gaze on Galen. "You have not expressed an opinion, Your Grace."

"Perhaps because I don't possess one," he replied evenly.

"I am sorry to hear that from a man of your influence."

He leaned back and regarded her thoughtfully. "You think I am a man of some influence?"

"You are a duke. Of course you have influence. Surely you must agree that exploiting one's employees and using the labor of children is, at the very least, false economy," Verity insisted, fighting her disappointment in his response.

"I must say I can believe that young workers and employees poorly paid will not give one a good day's labor."

"Well, be that as it may, I don't understand all this talk of mills and false economy for a moment—and I don't think we ladies should have to," Eloise said as she rose.

"We shall leave that to you men along with your brandy and cigars. Won't we, Verity, my dear?" she finished, giving her friend a very pointed and chastising look, which was not nearly so upsetting as Galen's responses, or having her family's past brought to light.

Perhaps Galen Bromney was not the man she had come to believe him to be, Verity thought, if he could not be incensed by the evils perpetrated in the mills, or if he saw and did not care—and that was worse.

"Forgive me, Sir Myron, for speaking so vehemently," Verity said as she, too, rose. "This is, after all, a social occasion, not a parliamentary debate."

After the ladies had departed in a rustle of silk, velvet and bombazine, Blackstone sighed patronizingly and addressed his host. "Ah, women! They would wish the world a rose garden, although they never consider that there would have to be pruning and manure."

"And some of us are more familiar with manure than others," Galen noted.

"We cannot all be aristocrats. Some of us must dirty our hands with trade," Blackstone said, still smiling with his lips.

However, the animosity in his eyes was all too apparent, and Galen almost felt sorry for the man. If he wanted to succeed in business, he should govern his expression better.

Not that Galen wanted Blackstone or others of his ilk to succeed, not when it meant the exploitation of his laborers. If it had not been for Verity's strictures about hiding their relationship, he would gladly have told her brother-in-law exactly what he thought of him and his systematic abuse of the weak.

In fact, he would be really quite delighted to see a man like Blackstone fail, and not just because of his business practices.

It was becoming increasingly obvious that Clive Blackstone's feelings for his widowed sister-in-law were far from brotherly. For that alone, Galen would gladly have banished him to the Outer Hebrides or the farthest, coldest reaches of Russia.

More unfortunately, Galen could believe that, with her sheltered existence, Verity was too naive to realize that. He, however, had spent long hours with cads and scoundrels, and he could easily recognize the possessive lust burning in Clive's beady eyes.

Restricted by Verity's admonitions and fear of scandal, it had been agonizing to watch the man and keep silent, as well as attend to Lady Mary as a dutiful suitor might.

Still, he was thankful to Blackstone for one thing: he had revealed the shadow in Verity's past that made her fearful of scandal and shame. While the slave trade still existed, for years now many people considered it a distasteful way to make money.

''If one wants to make a tidy sum these days, I can think of nothing better than a cotton mill,''

Blackstone continued. "After all, there is no such thing as too much wealth, eh, Your Grace? Sir Myron?"

"No, no, I suppose not," Myron mumbled uncertainly as he rose. "Brandy, anyone?"

Blackstone nodded and left the table.

As Galen joined them at the decanter, he said, "Sometimes it is better to be poor than earn one's money dishonorably."

Blackstone's lip curled slightly. "An interesting notion, coming as it does from one whose family got their estate from the seizure of Catholic lands in the days of Henry the Eighth."

"That was well before my time," Galen replied, only slightly impressed that Blackstone knew that. His family's past was not exactly a secret, and many noble families owed their estates, or portions of them, to the dissolution of Catholic monasteries, abbeys and convents.

"And you are such a fine example of aristocratic honor yourself."

Myron stepped between them and held up two glasses of brandy that shimmered in the candlelight. "Your brandy, gentlemen."

"Thank you," Blackstone muttered, while Galen accepted his with a nod.

"I believe we should join the ladies," Myron

suggested after he downed his drink in a hurried gulp. "Don't you agree, Galen?"

"Absolutely," he replied after wetting his lips.

He didn't want to overimbibe. He dared not, or he was surely going to tell this cursed Blackstone who dared to lust after Verity exactly what he thought of him and then challenge him to a duel.

Charging out of the dining room like a boar roused by beaters, Myron led the way to the drawing room. Blackstone didn't linger, either. Galen, however, took his time following, for he wanted to regain some measure of calm and self-control.

When he reached the drawing room, he immediately and instinctively sought out Verity. He quickly spotted her seated at Myron's pianoforte, a rather incongruous piece of furniture for his hunting lodge. Galen suspected it had come with the house and hadn't been played in years, for it definitely needed tuning.

Nevertheless, he enjoyed watching Verity play, even if he could only do so for a moment. Her face was illuminated by a candelabra she must have moved there herself; the glow and the bending of her head over the keys made her look like a Madonna. She moved gracefully as she played a light and charming air, with no music to guide her.

He could have watched her for hours, waiting for the occasional little wrinkle of concentration between her delicately arched brows to show itself again, or for the light to flicker over her lovely cheeks.

Suppressing a sigh, Galen strolled toward the other ladies.

Fanny Blackstone sat so rigidly, she might have had one of the pokers from the hearth up the back of her bodice. Clive hovered nearby and Myron stood awkwardly by the mantel as if not quite sure what to do, even though this was his house. Eloise reclined on the sofa like Cleopatra on her barge, playing with a loose string from her side hem, and Lady Mary perched on another chair nearby, smiling shyly.

She was always smiling shyly.

"I never had the pleasure of hearing Mrs. Davis-Jones play at Potterton Abbey," Galen observed.

Clive's gaze darted to Verity. "You never said the duke was at Potterton Abbey."

Verity glanced up. "Didn't I?"

"Is she regularly required to tell you about everybody she meets when she travels?"

"No, of course not."

"Oh, I beg your pardon."

"Lovely, simply lovely!" Eloise declared as the song ended. "George will be sorry he missed it."

"Is anybody else finding this room rather close?" Galen asked. "Lady Mary?"

"Yes," she ventured, her cheeks flushing.

Eloise gave Galen a pleased look that made him want to gnash his teeth. Instead, he sauntered toward the terrace door, which happened to be behind the piano.

"Myron, why don't you tell the ladies about your pineapples?" he suggested.

"Oh, indeed!" his friend cried happily. Then he launched into his favorite subject, after hunting, fishing, dogs, horses and guns.

As Galen drew closer, Verity's fingers fumbled over the keys, but nobody else seemed to notice.

He felt anxious, too, being so close to her and yet unable to touch her.

After he opened the terrace door a little, he turned and his glance encountered the exposed nape of Verity's slender neck.

He was astonishingly tempted to kiss her there.

Gad, perhaps it had been a mistake to come this close to her—yet this might be the best chance he would have to speak with her.

Ensuring that Myron still had his audience's attention for the time being, yet mindful that that would surely wander once he got into the particulars of the pineapple, he ventured closer to her.

Before he could say anything, however, she whispered, "Your Grace, I must speak to you. Privately. Tomorrow, if possible."

"Of course."

Even though this was what he himself had hoped to accomplish this evening, he felt a shiver of dread at her solemn tone.

"Can you meet me in the wood after the noon?"

"Yes."

"How very interesting, Sir Myron!" Eloise suddenly cried. "I had no idea the pineapple was such a *fascinating* fruit! Now, what do you say to some cards?"

"Cards?" Myron replied, obviously caught off guard.

"Cards. Whist, perhaps?"

"I should enjoy a game of whist," Lady Mary seconded.

"I know how to play whist," Myron replied, his pineapples obviously forgotten. "I'll have a table set out, shall I? Mr. and Mrs. Blackstone, will you play?"

Blackstone smiled his disgusting smile. "We would be delighted."

"We are too many for one table of whist," Galen noted as he reluctantly moved away from the piano, "and not enough for two."

"My wife will sit out," Blackstone offered.

"I would prefer to continue here, playing Sir Myron's lovely pianoforte," Verity said. "I am not good at cards."

"While I shall content myself with interfering with Lady Mary's play," Galen said, "if she can abide my presence."

"I would be grateful for your assistance, Your Grace," Lady Mary said, "for I fear I am not good with cards, either."

"Perhaps you are better at other games?" Galen suggested softly as a footman moved a round table and chairs for the players.

As Lady Mary blushed, Verity continued to play as if she were deaf and blind to anything but the piano.

Chapter Twelve

The next day, Galen glanced out the window of his bedchamber as he drew on his well-polished Hessians. Thank God the weather had cleared. It had rained all last night, and this morning had been foggy and damp.

He had not told Rhodes he was going out. Nor was he taking his horse. He was going to creep out of the house via the back stairs and past the forcing garden, doing his utmost to avoid any servants, who should be at their dinner.

He didn't know what Verity wanted to see him about, but he knew it must be important for her to risk a rendezvous—perhaps as important as what he had to say to her.

All night he had tossed and turned wondering if she wanted to confess that her feelings for him had changed, maybe even deepened into love, just as his feelings for her had altered.

There were, unfortunately, other possible explanations for her request.

It could be something as simple as an alteration in the time of his next visit with Jocelyn, given that the Blackstones were in Jefford. Perhaps she would bring Jocelyn with her.

Maybe Jocelyn was unwell—no, surely not, or Verity would never have left her to come to a dinner party.

Whatever the reason, he had struggled with impatience and hope and dread ever since she had proposed this meeting.

At last, however, it was finally time to leave and put an end to the questions and uncertainty.

After ensuring that the corridor was empty, he went out, locking his bedchamber door after him. When he returned, he would explain that he had been tired and taken a nap so that he would be refreshed for the evening. He had locked the door so he wouldn't be disturbed.

His plan of departure worked so successfully he thought it was a pity he had not considered a career in the foreign service as a spy.

Unfortunately, that would have required him to have some ambition in his youth, and he had possessed none.

Refusing to brood upon what might have been, Galen hurried along the path through the woods until he could make out Verity's house in the distance. Fearing he had come too close and might be seen, he stepped from the path behind some elderberry bushes to wait. He was also mindful of Rhodes and his desire to keep his activity secret, so he was careful not to brush against the wet leaves or berries. Otherwise, Rhodes would surely notice.

The scent of the damp earth and leaves reminded him of a cemetery, adding to his sense of foreboding. He looked at the dripping trees and watched as a crabapple fell to the soft ground. Cushioned by the humus, it barely made a sound.

Somewhere in the distance, a woodpecker began a search for bugs. Other birds sang, and a slight breeze stirred the branches, making more drips fall, their slow patter reminding him of a death knell.

Why was he so full of mournful thoughts? It must be the climate. He was not used to such gray skies and wet weather after his years in sunny Italy. Surely that would color a man's ruminations.

A twig snapped behind him and he glanced around quickly. Nothing. A squirrel probably, or a badger.

Gad, here he was in an English wood on a cool damp day, and he was sweating.

He wondered what Guido and the other villagers were doing back in Italy. Had they had a good harvest? Were they still arguing about the statue for the square? They couldn't decide on which saint it should be, although popular opinion seemed to be heading in favor of St. Michael.

Did they ever mention the solitary Englishman, or wonder when he would return?

When *would* he return? He had no idea, and would have none until he knew how Verity felt.

Then his love appeared, swathed in a long dark cloak, her expression grave and worried. Jocelyn was not with her, and although he would have enjoyed another visit with her, he was pleased that Verity was alone. He didn't want to make a declaration of love with an audience, especially when he wasn't absolutely sure of its reception.

"Verity!" he called out softly.

She halted, then held up her hand to stop him when he began to step out. "It will be better if you stay there, in case someone comes along the path," she replied quietly.

"Is that very likely? Perhaps we should go somewhere else."

He thought of the carriage house, and the kiss they had shared.

"This will have to do, but we must be careful. I will sit here, with my back to you."

Her choice of seat was a stone, kept mostly dry by a sheltering tree.

At her cool tone, more dread shivered down Galen's spine. "I don't want to talk to your back."

"It will be...easier," she answered in a whisper that he had to strain to hear.

"Why?"

Verity's shoulders rose and fell with a sigh. "Galen, I have come to the conclusion that it is simply too much of a risk for you to see us anymore."

His stomach knotted. "What do you mean, anymore?"

"I mean, I think you shouldn't visit us ever again."

Her words hurt more than any physical blow could have.

He marched around to stare at her. "Why not?"

She rose quickly. "It is too dangerous! People may suspect."

"Your servant didn't act as if she found anything amiss, nor have your in-laws. If they do not—"

"Not this time, perhaps, but they might find it very odd indeed if you keeping visiting us." She looked away and her voice fell. "You do resemble Jocelyn, you know."

"Perhaps it takes a mother's eyes to see it."

She lifted her head, and her eyes flashed with resolution. "Or more than one meeting."

"Maybe not."

"Even then, I cannot chance it. You have seen

my in-laws. You can guess how Clive will act if he finds out the truth.''

''What do you think he will do?''

Although her eyes continued to shine with a defiant gaze, her lip trembled. ''You're a man. What do you think he will do when he discovers his sister-in-law, who he pants after like a beast in heat, is not as virtuous as he suspects? What do you think he will ask her to do to ensure his silence?''

''I didn't think you knew how he—''

''Lusted after me? I am not a fool, Galen. And what weapon do you think I have wielded since my husband died to keep him distant? The shield of my supposed virtue. If that fails, he will not hesitate to use my secret against me, and Jocelyn, too.''

''Yet if his wife knows—''

''You've seen the way it is between them. He can tell her any lie he likes, and she won't question it.''

''Is there no way to be rid of the Blackstones?''

She shook her head. ''No. If anything happens to me, they must be Jocelyn's guardians. They are her nearest living relatives.''

''I do not like the idea of anything happening to you.''

She swallowed hard. ''I shall do my best to prevent it, I promise you.''

''But if it does, Jocelyn has me.''

"Not legally."

"I would change that if I could. That man is a greedy, disgusting lout."

"You didn't seem to find fault with his business practices."

"I kept silent because of your wish to avoid any hint of a relationship between us, but I assure you, Verity, I do not excuse what goes on in the name of business these days. In fact, I have refused to invest in such enterprises for years, and I give financial aid to those who legally seek to improve the conditions of the workers."

She relaxed a little. "I am glad to hear that, Galen, and I do appreciate that you've tried to keep our secret. Nevertheless, we cannot continue in this way."

"I have lost you once, and that was enough," Galen said, his voice hoarse with suppressed emotion. "I don't want to lose you, or Jocelyn, ever again. Verity, I love you. I want us to be together, as a family, with our daughter."

She put her gloved finger against his lips, as she had touched him so long ago, but oh, how different was the expression in her eyes now!

Before, they had been full of yearning and desire; today, he saw anguish—and stern resolution. "Please, Galen, don't."

"Don't love you? Good God, Verity, don't you think I tried not to? You left me without a word of explanation and let me live with that for ten years. You bore my child and never told me. You married another man. How *could* I love you?"

Her eyes filled with tears. "The same way I could love you," she proposed softly, "despite all rational reasons I should not."

He stared at her with undisguised happiness. "You love me? Oh, God, Verity! And I love you!"

With a gasp of joy, he pulled her into his arms and kissed her hungrily, with all the passion she inspired.

She twisted away. "No, Galen, don't! Don't make this more difficult for me—for us. We *cannot* see each other again."

"Because you fear scandal and rumors and gossip." He reached out and took her gently by the shoulders, gazing at her intensely. "Verity, I am a duke, and as you said last night, I have influence. I can shield you—"

"No, you can't!"

"Verity," he began again, determined to make her listen. Resolved to make her agree. "I know that you have had to live with a certain notoriety, given your father's failings and the family business but—"

"A *certain* notoriety?" she repeated, pulling away. "Because of my father and my family's involvement in the slave trade?"

"Yes, and—"

"Oh, Galen if only that were all! That is not the worst of it."

"There is more?" he asked, a horrible dread sickening him.

Had his not been the first bed she had sought? Had there been other men afterward, other lovers?

"I am a bastard, the offspring of an adulterous relationship."

He waited a long moment. "Is that all?"

"All?" she repeated, eyeing him curiously. "Is that not—"

She gasped and colored, even as anger filled her eyes.

"Forgive me, Verity," Galen cried. "I was...afraid."

"Afraid? Afraid that you had fallen in love with a woman little better than a whore?"

"No," he declared softly, looking at her with grim resolution. "Afraid I would not compare favorably with other men, in any way, beyond my title and notoriety."

"Galen, I have only loved two men in my life— you, and Daniel, whom I loved more as a father than a husband."

"Verity, if you love me, I fear nothing."

Despite the tender fervor in his eyes, she willed herself to continue. He could not know what it was like to be a bastard in English society, and she had to convince him that she knew whereof she spoke.

"Galen, I will tell you what my life was like before I married Daniel.

"Other people knew about my dishonorable parentage long before I was privy to the family secret. They would whisper and point and sneer, as if something was wrong with me. As if I had committed a great and terrible sin, and that I was not acting with appropriate contrition.

"But how could I?" she demanded, all her old frustration and resentment rising in her. "I didn't know what was wrong. Then slowly, gradually, I discovered all—*all*—that my family tried to hide. I found out why my father didn't love me, why he could hardly bear to look at me, and why he sought solace in a bottle."

She clasped her hands together fervently. "Galen, I *know* what it is like to be always on the fringe of society, never quite belonging, always set apart through no fault of one's own.

"You say being a duke will protect us, but you know the ways of the ton—or you should. They may be somewhat more subtle, but they will be just as cruel.

"And when Jocelyn is a young woman, what will the men think? I know full well. Like mother, like daughter. She will be propositioned and pursued as if she were little better than a harlot."

Verity's voice dropped to a low whisper. "She

may even think that of herself and give herself to men she does not love, for passion or security.''

She came closer to him, gazing steadily at him with her determined blue eyes. ''I will not subject my daughter to that. If you care for her at all, you won't wish it upon her, either.''

''I do care for her, and that is why I cannot dismiss her from my life. I am willing to play the role of family friend, if that will content you.''

''And I have explained to you, people may guess that at one time, you were more than that to me.'' Her eyes pleaded with him to understand. ''You must do as I ask, for Jocelyn's sake.''

''Is there no way I could see her, not even at school?''

''I will never send Jocelyn away to school.''

''She is a clever child and should have every opportunity my money can afford, Verity. I will make my financial contributions in secret, and her relationship to me can remain unknown.''

''No. I will not send her away. She has had enough upheaval in her life.'' Verity's steadfast gaze faltered. ''Besides, I would be too lonely without her. She is all I have.''

''Yet you think nothing of condemning me to loneliness. Without...'' He hesitated a moment. ''Without Jocelyn, I have no one.''

''You have many friends, many interests,'' Verity replied. ''And I think, before long, you will have a wife. Then, later, other children. You will forget—''

''About you and Jocelyn? Never! I never forgot you before, try as I might, and now that I know about my daughter, I will not banish her from my life.''

She reached out and took his hand. ''Nevertheless, you must try to do just that. You must make a new life, Galen, and forget the past.''

His fingers tightened around hers as his gaze searched her face. ''And you? Will you make a new life, or will you continue to hide yourself away, with only Jocelyn and Nancy for company?''

Her head bowed and a tear fell to the ground.

''I love you, Verity! I do not want to live a new life if you are not in it! Please do not send me away. I love you. I need you. I want to marry you!''

Galen took her in his arms and kissed her.

As his tender yet insistent lips moved upon hers, she did not fight the desire of her heart and yearning for his love.

A low moan escaped her throat as she gave in to her desire.

''Oh, God, Verity,'' he murmured as he dragged his lips across her flushed cheek. ''I have only just found you again.''

It took the memory of every veiled insult, every

sly insinuation and scornful glance, to make her pull away.

"It must be this way, Galen, for our daughter's sake," she said. "It must be."

"You will not marry me?"

"No."

His voice dropped to a distraught whisper. "You said you loved me, yet you are willing to abandon me again."

Her eyes shone with something more than tears as she raised her head and looked at him. "There is only one person who I love as much as you, Galen, and that is Jocelyn. It is only for her sake I ask this. For her, I would break your heart—and my own."

"Verity!"

"Please, Galen, go," she whispered, needing every ounce of her resolve and concern for her daughter's welfare to say it.

He reached out to take hold of her shoulders. "If I must never see you again, for our daughter's sake, let me tell you once more how I love you."

"Galen, please, it is too much," she stammered, holding him away from her. "I cannot bear it."

"Then let me kiss you again."

"Galen," she protested feebly as he drew her close.

She did not have the strength to refuse. She did not want to refuse.

This kiss was gentle, tender and tasted of the salt of her tears.

With a ragged sigh, he stepped back. "May I write to you?"

"That would not be wise."

"Will you write to me in London to tell me how you and Jocelyn are?" he pleaded. "No one in my household will wonder if I get a letter addressed in a lady's hand."

Hearing his mournful, heartfelt words, she could not refuse his request. "I shall write, Galen, but it cannot be often. I will have to find a way to post it in secret, but I shall write. I give you my word."

He grasped her hand and raised it to his lips. "Then I shall be content, or try to be."

"And so must I." She drew her hand away. "What of Lady Mary?"

"Oh, yes. Lady Mary." He shrugged. "Perhaps…in time…when I am able to contemplate marriage to anyone but you…"

He abruptly turned and strode a few paces away, then just as suddenly halted and looked back. "Goodbye, Verity. Give my love to Jocelyn."

She nodded.

He wheeled around and marched down the path. Around the bend.

And out of her life. Again. Forever.

She wanted to moan with despair, or scream in agony. She wanted to weep and wail, gnash her teeth, tear her hair.

But most of all, she wanted to call him back to her.

She did none of these things, for she would not make her daughter suffer for *her* happiness.

So instead, after several minutes had elapsed, Verity wiped her eyes, sighed heavily, straightened her shoulders and headed back to her house.

She did not see the man behind the oak on the other side of the path who had watched and listened, a dark scowl marring his familiar features.

"London?" Myron said with a snort, coming out of doze and half out of his chair as he stared at Galen, with whom he had been sharing a companionable moment of calm in the drawing room before the ladies—and possibly George—came down for dinner.

"Yes. I'm sorry, Myron, yet I fear I must return immediately. Tomorrow, in fact. There is some business I have only just remembered, no doubt because I've had such an enjoyable time here."

"Thanks to Lady Mary, eh?"

Galen forced a noncommittal smile onto his face and remained enigmatically silent.

"Well, if you must, you must. I'm dashed grateful you came down at all."

"Myron, it is I who am grateful," Galen replied truthfully. "And I'm very sorry indeed I never came before."

If he had, perhaps he would have encountered Verity and Jocelyn sooner, and maybe he could have found a way to be part of their lives. Somehow.

Regrettably, he could never come here again, because he did not think he had the strength to stay away from them if he was so nearby.

"You must promise to visit me when you come to London," Galen said.

Now that he had regained his friendship with Myron and valued it as he always should have, he didn't want to lose that, too.

And it could very well be that Myron might be able to give him additional news of Verity and Jocelyn from time to time.

"That's very kind of you," Myron said.

He was so obviously delighted, Galen felt another twinge of guilt for not inviting him before this.

Then Myron frowned. "The ladies are going to be very disappointed you're leaving us."

"I think you overestimate my attraction."

"Do I? I'm sure Lady Mary has been entertaining certain hopes."

"Led on by my own esteemed cousin, surely.

Still, I am not saying that she need be disappointed."

"And here I was really wondering if you were contemplating the pretty widow," Myron said sheepishly.

Galen managed a wry laugh. "No, no widows for me, thank you."

Myron seemed relieved, and a new thought came to Galen.

What if Myron were interested in Verity?

No, it couldn't be. It mustn't be.

Yet if Verity were to marry anybody, even Myron, that would free her from her in-laws. If he wanted her to be free—and he did—he should even encourage that. As for Myron, he was a good, kind, generous soul.

Despite such reasoning, Galen felt physically ill at the thought of Verity married to anybody except himself.

Perhaps he was leaping to conclusions unnecessarily.

"Mrs. Davis-Jones is pretty, of course," he remarked. "Have you taken a fancy to her?"

"Demme, no!" Myron cried, truly horrified. Then he blushed like a boy telling a dirty story.

"I thought you didn't believe those rumors about her husband's death," Galen asked, searching for a possible explanation for Myron's reaction.

"Oh, that. No, I don't."

"What then?"

"She's not…that is, her mother…"

Galen's jaw tensed. "What is the matter?"

"Well, in my last letter to Justbury Minor I told him that you had come down and I mentioned my pretty bereaved neighbor. Today I received a reply. I fear I have been noticing somebody I should not, and I must say I'm rather shocked your cousin does, although I suppose the old school ties may be just as strong with the weaker sex."

"What the devil are you talking about, Myron?"

His friend blushed. "It seems, um, that Mrs. Davis-Jones is not the child of her mother's husband."

Deep in his heart, Galen had wanted to believe that Verity was exaggerating the stain of illegitimacy, but if kindhearted, jovial Myron could look as if he had just revealed that Verity was a multiple murderer, what would other people be like? Other men?

"Since she seems to be a gentle, demure woman, and since I know how rumors can run rampant with very little encouragement," Galen replied, "I hope you won't feel called upon to repeat what you have heard. There is her innocent child to consider, too."

"Yes, yes, you're right," Myron acknowledged, and Galen subdued a sigh of relief.

If he prevented even one person from spreading the story of Verity's past, that would be something.

At the sound of rustling skirts and Eloise's exclamations, Myron got to his feet and gruffly cleared his throat. "I'll let you disappoint the ladies and tell them that you're leaving us."

"Of course."

With a subdued sigh, Galen turned to greet Eloise, who fluttered in with an aura of lacy bits and perfume, her chartreuse evening gown both ugly and revealing. Lady Mary, much more tastefully attired in pale pink silk and with a single rose in her hair, entered with her.

"You both look enchanting," Galen said.

Lady Mary's smile grew a little bolder and she sidled a little closer. Really, one would think he was a wolf, the way she behaved when she was near him, Galen thought with sudden irritation.

"Thank you, thank you!" Eloise gushed as she sat on the edge of the sofa and adjusted her glove. "That is more than George ever says. Indeed, I could stand in front of him naked and he wouldn't say a thing."

Struck dumb, no doubt, was Galen's first thought. "Where is he?"

"Still trying to get his cravat tied properly," Eloise replied. "Your man Rhodes has come to his aid, so we should be seeing him soon enough."

Galen decided he had better get his announcement over with. "I am sorry to say that I shall be leaving for London very early in the morning. If you ladies have any commission for me there, or wish me to convey any messages, I shall be delighted to do so."

Lady Mary looked stunned, and Eloise frowned as darkly as she could.

"You must stay as long as you like, Lady Bodenham, Lady Mary," Myron hastened to add. "Indeed, after all the excitement of having such marvelous company, I shall turn as growly as a bear if you decamp, too!"

"Whatever can there be to make you leave in such a rush?" Eloise demanded.

"Estate business," Galen replied simply.

The less said, the better.

"I thought your man Jasper handled all that."

"He cannot sign my name on legal documents," Galen replied.

This was quite true, although it had nothing to do with his return to London.

"Oh, well, then," Eloise said grudgingly as she reclined on the sofa.

"We shall miss you, Your Grace," Lady Mary ventured.

"I hope we can renew our acquaintance at a later date, Lady Mary," he replied gallantly.

When he saw her pleased smile, the noose tightened more.

Chapter Thirteen

The next morning, as Verity made some desultory efforts to sweep the kitchen floor before Nancy returned from the market in the village, she tried not to remember Galen and his culinary efforts. She would not shed tears when she moved the little pot in which he had boiled an egg, and she would not wax sentimental over the cloth that had protected his fingers.

The door burst open, breaking her reverie, and Nancy came bustling in. She set her basket on the table and, with arms akimbo and bonnet askew, regarded her mistress as an overseer might an insolent workman. "*What* do you think has happened now?"

"I have no idea," Verity answered as she laid her broom against the wall, "but please speak softly. The Blackstones are not yet awake."

Nancy cast a scornful glance ceilingward, then

turned her attention back to Verity. "You'll never guess."

"I think you're right, so please tell me."

"He's up and left!"

Verity went to the table and began to empty the basket of the few items Nancy had purchased. "Who?"

"The Duke of Deighton—and his precious Titus Minimus!"

Judging by the way she had tossed things into the basket, Nancy had been irritated from the start of her marketing.

"Why should that upset you?" Verity inquired. "Did you get the flour?"

"Because folks couldn't stop talking about it, even with me standing there waiting to pay good money to 'em! And as for that Jill at the mill!" Nancy relieved her feelings by turning around and shaking her fist in the general direction of Jefford. "You'd think he'd jilted her at the altar, the hussy!"

"Who, the duke or his valet?"

"Either one—or both, the jade! Took me an age to get her to measure the flour out."

"Oh, yes, here it is." Verity returned the empty basket to its place by the door. "Well, if he is gone, things should soon return to normal. Is Lady Bodenham still at Sir Myron's?"

"I suppose so. They didn't say she'd gone, or

that other one, either. O' course, they wouldn't have taken no notice of that unless they'd sprouted wings and flown over their heads!''

''Is that Nancy?'' Jocelyn called from the parlor.

''Yes, she's home.''

''Good. The duke would like to speak to her, too,'' Jocelyn said.

Verity had to lean on the table for support. ''Who?''

''The duke. I've just let him in!''

How could he do this? After all she had said... explained...made clear...how could he disregard her wishes so blatantly?

What if he meant to continue disregarding them? He was a duke, a rich and powerful nobleman. She would have little means to prevent him.

She glanced at Nancy to see an equally dismayed and suspicious look on her face.

''Well, this is certainly a surprise,'' Verity said with forced gaiety. ''To have a duke take leave of *me!*'' She lowered her voice to a confidential whisper. ''You know, I fear you may have been right all along about him. I am so relieved he's leaving Jefford!''

''No doubt that Jill will think he's lingering on after *her*, and her with them buckteeth.''

''Let us say our goodbyes quickly, then.''

She hurried to the parlor, Nancy behind her.

For the first time, the sight of Galen and his

charming smile failed to move her. All she could think of was his selfish disregard for the risk he was taking by coming here.

"Good morning, Your Grace," she began coolly as she entered the parlor.

"Good morning, and pray forgive the early hour of my call."

"He says he's come to say goodbye," Jocelyn said, and Verity noted the tears welling her daughter's eyes, and her trembling lip.

She was doing all she could not to cry.

Verity glanced sharply at Galen—and in that instant, her anger dissolved. He was looking at Jocelyn with both intensity and torment, as if he were trying to memorize her features and trying not to cry, too.

She knew then he had not come to make threats or plead with her to change her mind. He had come to see his daughter for what might be the last time.

"I couldn't go without saying farewell to you all. I shall never forget your kindness and hospitality," he said. He smiled, but it was empty of any joy.

"Well, you're welcome and goodbye, then," Nancy snapped from the doorway, where she regarded him with obvious suspicion.

"You'll come back, won't you?" Jocelyn pleaded. "You'll come to visit Sir Myron again, won't you? Next time, I can show you how to toast bread.''

''We shall see.''

''Jocelyn, the duke has many claims upon his time.''

''And he's got to get on his way now, no doubt,'' Nancy finished. ''Folks to visit, estates to run, parties to attend, the House of Lords to snore in.''

''Nancy, I am so glad you are here. I have a very great favor to ask of you,'' Galen said, smiling at her with some genuine good humor and not a little forbearance.

''A favor of me, Your Grace?'' she replied dubiously.

''I should dearly love to have the recipe for the tarts. I know that no one will be able to make them as well as you two, but perhaps my chef in London can achieve a near proximity. Will you be so generous as to let me have it?''

''It ain't—isn't—written down. I keep it here,'' she replied, tapping her temple.

''Perhaps you could write it out at some later date and send it on to me at London? Here is my address.'' He reached into his pocket and pulled out a card. ''Mrs. Davis-Jones, if you would be so good as to pass this to Nancy?''

Of course, Verity thought as she reached out to take the card, her hand touching his for the briefest

of moments. She would have to have Galen's address if she were to write. Otherwise, she would
have to get it from Eloise or Sir Myron, and that
would involve more subterfuge and complications.
It was much easier to read it on the card and com-
mit it to memory as she handed it to Nancy.

"Perhaps the duke would appreciate some tarts
for his journey? Jocelyn and Nancy made a fresh
batch yesterday."

"That would be delightful."

"They're even better than the ones you had before," Jocelyn assured him.

"Nancy, would you be so good as to get him
some?"

Nancy nodded. "All right. I'll say my goodbye,
then, Your Grace. Goodbye."

"Goodbye, Nancy."

She nodded briskly once, then exited the room,
leaving Galen alone with Verity and Jocelyn.

He knew it would be better if he left at once.
He didn't doubt that the longer he lingered, the
greater the pain would be when he eventually tore
himself away. But he had to come one more time
to ensure that Verity knew his London address, and
because he couldn't bear the thought of not saying
a final farewell to Jocelyn.

With a woeful smile, he looked down into Jocelyn's eyes that were so like her mother's and
touched one dark curl that was so like his.

"I have to go now, Jocelyn," he said softly. "I have a long day's journey ahead, made somewhat better by the offer of the tarts."

"We never played Indians."

"No."

She gave him a look as serious and studious as an adult's. "Why are you really going away?"

He heard Verity's sharp intake of breath, but ignored it. "Because I must. Sometimes people must do things they would rather not."

"But you're a *duke* and rich, too."

Before Verity could say anything, Galen answered, "That does not mean I have no obligations, Jocelyn. I would rather stay a little longer, but I simply cannot."

Suddenly they heard noises overheard. Galen glanced at Verity and realized she had tensed. "I don't think that's a mouse," he ventured.

"It's Uncle Clive and Aunt Fanny," Jocelyn announced. "They've been asleep all morning."

"It is not yet ten o'clock," Verity reminded her. "Your Grace, do you wish to take your leave of them, too?"

"Sadly, I have overstayed my time as it is," Galen replied.

He didn't want to see the Blackstones again, especially Clive, because he didn't trust himself not to warn the man to keep away from Verity on pain of death.

Galen crouched down until he was eye to eye with the daughter he yearned to acknowledge, and to know. "Goodbye, Jocelyn. I hope to hear your war whoop again someday."

Her lip started to tremble again. "Goodbye," she mumbled. Then she ran out of the room. They heard her feet pounding up the stairs and a door banged shut.

"I'm sorry, Galen," Verity whispered as he straightened, "but it has to be this way."

He sighed heavily and gave her a weary shadow of his smile. "I know."

He reached out and took her hand gently. "I only wish—" he began gruffly, as if his words would come out of his throat despite a manly effort to keep silent.

"Will you...can you...perhaps someday, when she is old enough to understand, will you tell her the truth?"

Verity nodded slowly.

"Please do not make me sound too much a rake, if that is not too much to ask."

"I shall tell her what a good and unselfish man her natural father was," Verity vowed.

Nancy appeared in the drawing room door, a cloth bundle in her hand, and Galen raised Verity's hand to his lips for a kiss. "Goodbye, Mrs. Davis-Jones."

"Farewell, Your Grace," she whispered as she curtsied.

Then he walked toward Nancy, took the bundle, gave Verity a final, enigmatic glance, and left.

"Goodbye and good riddance to 'im!" Nancy muttered as she closed the door behind him. "All charm and flattery, that one."

Verity opened her mouth, ready to tell Nancy that she was wrong. Quite wrong. There was so much more to him than that.

And so much more that she wished to learn.

But he was gone.

He was gone forever.

"I don't see that he was so very handsome," Nancy muttered as she headed to the kitchen. "What with that hair and them manners, looking at you like he'd like to take a bite out o' you."

Verity reached for her shawl hanging on a peg near the door. "I am going to the woods for a walk, Nancy. I shouldn't be long."

She didn't wait to hear Nancy's response.

She fled to the solitude of the woods.

A few days later, Galen sat in the library of his Mayfair town house, staring unseeing into the flames in the hearth. Heavy plum-colored velvet draperies covered the windows, so no street noise penetrated the silence. He had not bothered to light any candles. The door was closed, and the servants knew better than to disturb him there.

Between the draperies, the dark paneling and lack of illumination, the library was as dim as a tomb, and Galen liked it that way.

He sighed and ran his hand through his unkempt hair. He hadn't gone out today, and he wasn't going out tonight. He would rather sit in his library alone.

He glanced at the letter from Eloise lying open on his desk. It seemed Lady Mary was going to be in London next month.

He stood abruptly, poured himself a brandy and downed it in a gulp. Gad, he didn't want to marry her! He didn't want to marry anybody but Verity. He would never love any woman as he did her.

He strode to the desk and grabbed Eloise's letter. With fiendish relish he crumpled it into a little ball and tossed it toward the fireplace. It bounced off the bronze andiron and fell into the flames. Smiling with satisfaction, he watched as the edges caught fire, curled, blackened and disintegrated into ashes.

Then he sighed. ''That was mature,'' he muttered sardonically. ''And you thought you had become a more sensible man.''

He so dearly wished he had always been a sensible man! Then he would not be in this hellish exile of his own making. He would have been worthy of Verity's love from the beginning, and perhaps she wouldn't have married—

Such speculation was worthless. The past was the past. He could not undo what he had done, just as she could not. He must try to carry on.

He picked up the other letter that had been on his desk, written in Buck's familiar, yet obviously weak, hand.

There had been a time Galen would never have written to his half brother, not even to inquire how he fared after his illness. Having lost Jocelyn and Verity, however…well, he had written to all three of his brothers when he returned to London.

Buck had been quite ill with a fever and was slowly recovering. He didn't know when he would be back in England, and the tone of his shaky writing indicated he really didn't think Galen cared.

Buck was wrong. Galen was truly glad to hear that his half brother was doing better and would be coming home. Galen would wait to see him before he went back to Italy, and he would have War and Hunt come for a visit to London, too. If only he could add Verity and Jocelyn to that family gathering!

"Your Grace?"

"What it is?" he growled, turning toward the door.

"I did knock, Your Grace," a liveried footman

stammered as he held out a silver salver bearing a visiting card.

"I don't want to see anybody."

"He says it's very important, Your Grace, and was most insistent."

"Insistent?" Galen scoffed as he snatched up the card. "Who dares to be *insistent* to the Duke of Deighton?"

He frowned as he read the name in the flickering light of the hearth fire: Clive Blackstone.

He had absolutely no desire to see or talk to the obsequious Clive Blackstone. The man was probably going to ask him to invest in his mills again, something Galen would never do. "Tell him I am not at home."

"I'm sorry, Your Grace," the footman replied, blanching under Galen's angry glare. "He said if you refused to see him, I was to say it was about an extremely important personal matter...about a widow, Your Grace."

Galen's throat went dry. "Ask him to join me here."

After the footman left, he tried to compose himself. He told himself it was natural that Blackstone would refer to Verity. She had been to school with his cousin.

Clive Blackstone strolled into the library. Gone was the humble, fawning manner he had possessed in Jefford. Now the fellow boldly ignored Galen and let his gaze insolently rove over the multitude of richly bound volumes on the wall, the carpet and the fine cherry wood and leather furniture, as if he were an auctioneer Galen had summoned to sell off every piece.

Galen said nothing; nevertheless, he knew this change of manner did not bode well.

His perusal concluded, the man regarded Galen with a smile as he bowed. "Your Grace, I am so pleased you would see me."

"I was given to understand you have come on an important personal matter," Galen replied, using the frostiest tone he possessed.

The slyly smiling Blackstone did not answer right away. Instead, he sat down without waiting for an invitation to do so.

"What brings you here?" Galen demanded.

"Business, Your Grace, business. Of a very particular kind."

Galen didn't like the man's tone, either—smug and knowing, unpleasantly intimate. "Oh?"

The man's catlike smile widened. "It concerns my sister-in-law and her child."

"I must confess I fail to see why that would bring you to me."

"You know how much she cares for the child, don't you, Your Grace?" Blackstone replied. "As much as a parent could care for a child, I believe."

He spoke in a way that made Galen's eyes narrow and his jaw clench. "Yes, I gather she loves her daughter very much. What has that to do with me?"

Blackstone answered his query with another question. "And the child's father? How much does he care for her?"

Galen felt the cold trickle of sweat down his back. "That is an odd question, Mr. Blackstone. The child's father is dead."

Blackstone's smile grew as wide as it was possible for a smile to be and he leaned back into Galen's chair as if he were the master here. "Oh, is he?"

"Don't think to play games with me, Blackstone," Galen answered, his voice very quiet and very stern.

Blackstone sat up straighter, but that damnable smile didn't disappear. "I did not come all the way to London to play games, Your Grace. I assure you, my object is very serious. Very serious indeed."

"What *is* your object?"

"Sit down, Your Grace, and let us discuss my business as men of business should, calmly and rationally."

"Who do you think you are, to order me?"

Blackstone swallowed hard, but he did not look away. "I think I am a man who knows your greatest secret, and so your greatest weakness, just as I know my sister-in-law's.''

Galen struggled not to show any hint of the anger, disgust and dismay roiling through him—or the terrible and familiar feeling of utter helplessness.

But he was not a child anymore.

''Sit down, won't you, Your Grace?''

''I would rather stand.''

''Very well. I daresay we will come to terms quickly enough.''

''Terms? What terms? For what?''

''My financial terms, for keeping quiet about what I know.''

''Blackmail. I should have guessed,'' Galen muttered, his hatred for the man growing with every word Blackstone uttered and every minute he was in his presence.

''An ugly word, but appropriate,'' Blackstone acknowledged.

''What is it you think you know?''

''I know that Jocelyn Davis-Jones is your child, not my dear departed brother-in-law's.''

Galen made a derisive grunt. ''That's preposterous.''

''I have it on the best authority.''

''What authority?'' Galen scoffed. ''A genie? Some soothsayer? A gypsy, perhaps?''

''Verity told me.''

For an instant, Galen felt as if a rock had struck him in the stomach. Then his lip curled with renewed scorn. "You, sir, are the most outrageous liar I have ever had the misfortune to meet."

Blackstone didn't blink an eye. "You know otherwise, for you confirmed it, too, that day in the wood. Such passionate embraces, too." Blackstone's smile grew more feral.

Galen's hands bunched into fists. Was it possible they had been seen and overheard? He remembered the snap of the twig. Gad, he *had* been careless!

"I quite envy you, Your Grace, for that, and most especially the rest ten years ago. Or have there been other assignations I have not been privy to?"

"If there had been, I daresay you are sorry you were not there to spy upon them."

"Are you going to deny that Jocelyn is your daughter?"

Galen smiled a smile that should have given Blackstone pause. "No."

"I am glad of that."

"Why should I? Fathering a bastard is not a crime."

"But Verity doesn't want anybody to know, and since I do, how much are you willing to pay to prevent me from sharing what I know?"

"That would depend upon how many others you have already told."

"I haven't told anyone—yet. No, not even dear, sweet, lovely Verity."

She didn't know. Thank God, she didn't know.

"As for who I'd tell, Your Grace," Clive continued, "why, anyone and everyone I met."

"What proof would you offer? It would be your word against ours."

"Even without proof, people would believe it. What was her mother but an adulteress? What are you but a lascivious cad? Do you think people require a legal document to believe a rumor?"

Galen could not deny the truth of his assertion.

"Besides, Your Grace, the child does look like you."

"As you are so good to point out, I have very little reputation to lose, so there is no reason I should pay for your silence."

"Except for the sake of the people you love."

Galen had been thinking matrimony a noose; now, he was caught in an even more terrible trap, because Blackstone had found the one reason Galen would do what every particle of his being rebelled against. For Verity and Jocelyn's sake, he would do anything, even to putting himself in this loathsome man's power.

But not yet. Not until he was sure there was no other way. "Even if you destroy Verity's reputation, what profit would there be in that for you? Daniel Davis-Jones's will should still be legal and binding, so there would be no financial gain for you.''

''Legal and binding under those circumstances? Perhaps. Or perhaps it will take years for the lawyers to sort it out. And perhaps the sudden death of the betrayed husband will be reconsidered.''

''He died of pneumonia.''

Clive's grin was the most evil thing Galen had ever laid eyes on. ''Oh, did he?''

''You know that as well as I. The doctor saw nothing suspicious.''

''A jury of twelve good men and true might believe that a woman who had acted so disgracefully might be capable of anything.

''Besides, even if she is not guilty of any crime, the papers will enjoy the trial, I'm sure. A juicy bit for their readers, and with a duke in the story, too. Shall we try it, do you think?''

''You wouldn't dare. I could hire the best lawyers in England to defend her.''

''Of course you could,'' Blackstone replied with a patronizing sneer that twisted into another mocking grin. ''But in the meantime, my dear duke, think of the scandal. Verity will. You know her aversion to scandal, for the child's sake. I merely thought I would give you the chance to be her white knight. Rather a new role for the Duke of Deighton, eh?'' He chuckled softly. ''However, if you will not pay me to keep quiet, *she* will. Some-how."

With a growl of rage, Galen lunged for the man, hauled him out of the chair by the collar and worried him like a terrier. "If you so much as lay one hand on her, I'll kill you, by God!"

Chapter Fourteen

Clive struggled in Galen's grasp. "Do you want to add murderer to your reputation?" he gasped.

Galen let go, throwing the man back so he hit the shelves, sending down a cascade of books. Clive covered his head with his arms and cowered, while Galen tried to calm his ragged breathing.

There was a knock at the door. "Your Grace?" a footman inquired tentatively. "Is anything the matter?"

"Some books fell. Nothing serious," he replied as he continued to glare at Clive Blackstone, who stumbled to his feet and rubbed his throat.

"That wasn't wise," he whispered hoarsely.

His mouth hard, Galen glared at Blackstone. Every impulse within him urged him to tell this wretch to go to hell—but he could not.

Just as Verity had never been able to.

Galen had never admired her more than he did

now, when he realized how strong she was to deal with this odious creature, and still maintain such spirit and determination. "How much will it cost to send you and your wife from the country?"

"From the country?" Clive asked as he straightened his disheveled clothing.

"You heard me. How much will it cost me to get you out of England and keep you out of it?"

"I have my mills to think of—"

"I'll buy them. *How much?*"

The man's eyes gleamed greedily as he took a moment to consider. "Thirty thousand pounds."

Galen's chest tightened. He was wealthy, to be sure, but not in ready cash. This would totally deplete his bank account. But haggle with this man for Verity's security he would not.

"Very well." Galen strode to the desk. "I shall give you half now and deliver the other half to you personally aboard ship just before you sail."

He quickly wrote the necessary notes. "I have explained to my banker that I am going into the cotton business."

How he would later explain this temporary acquisition to Jasper he didn't know, and he didn't care. The most important thing was to protect Verity and Jocelyn.

His lip curling with scorn, he held out the papers as if they were diseased and the man accepting them leprous. "Don't even think of talking to Verity before you go. I hardly need remind you that I have an acquaintance in Jefford, and I can always find out from Sir Myron if she has had visitors. Now get out of my sight.''

Blackstone slowly perused the papers, then folded them and put them in his frock coat. ''A pleasure doing business with you, Your Grace. Not that I wouldn't have enjoyed the alternative—''

Galen took a step toward him. ''Never forget, Blackstone, that you are dealing with a duke, and one who has spent more time than he cares to remember with the lowlife of London. If you force my hand, if you so much as write to her, I swear you'll wish you'd never been born.''

Blackstone paled, then turned and scurried from the room like the rat he was.

After he had gone, Galen paced across the carpet, his gaze intensely fastened on the fabric beneath his feet, as if he were a weaver examining every thread.

In truth, he saw nothing. All his mind focused on was Blackstone and the threat he presented not to Galen, but to Verity and Jocelyn.

Would Blackstone stay away from them? To be sure, he had been frightened by Galen's threat, but later, would his arrogant belief in the power of the secret he possessed make him bold?

Galen could believe it would, especially if Verity was the prize.

Yet thirty thousand pounds—surely that would be sufficient impetus to do as Galen ordered.

But how many times had he heard of tales of blackmailers who took a sum of money, then asked for more and more? How long might the thirty thousand pounds content Blackstone? How long before he asked for more money, or went to Verity to demand…

Maybe not long at all. Maybe he would risk going to her as soon as he was out of London, trusting in Verity's determination to avoid scandal to keep such a visit a secret, too.

He should go to Verity at once and warn her.

What if he were wrong? What if Blackstone did take the money and do as he commanded? Warning Verity would only upset her, and for nothing.

That revelation might even frighten her so much she would flee with Jocelyn to someplace where he might never find them again. Under those circumstances, she probably wouldn't dare to write him.

He would be totally alone in the world, more so than ever before, because he would know what he had lost.

Galen sank to his knees. He felt so helpless, so utterly unsure of what he should do or where he should go.

''Oh, God, tell me what to do,'' he whispered.

"I want them to be safe, but I don't want to be alone."

Then he raised his head, a resolute expression on his face.

Galen Bromney, Duke of Deighton, who had run away and hid from his troubles for ten years, knew exactly what he had to do.

He had to warn Verity. He had to tell her Clive knew their secret and that he might try to use that knowledge against her.

And if that meant that Verity and Jocelyn disappeared so that he couldn't even hear of them from time to time, if that meant Verity would never write to him, he would have to risk that.

He would have her free of Clive Blackstone, no matter what the cost to him.

Blowing a loose bit of hair from her eyes, Verity briskly wrung out the rag, then again fell to scrubbing the hall near the door to the parlor. She didn't mind the sweat pouring down her back from her exertions, or the pain in her knees from kneeling on the hard wooden floor. Ever since Galen had left Jefford, she had cleaned and scrubbed and tidied as if her life depended upon a spotless house.

In a way, she supposed it did, because cleaning kept her busy and her mind occupied, and by nightfall, she was so tired, she fell into a dreamless, exhausted sleep.

Otherwise, she would lie awake thinking about Galen, and what might have been.

At the unexpected sound of a carriage, she stopped scrubbing and stood as quickly as her sore knees would let her. She wasn't expecting any visitors.

She took a few steps into the parlor and looked out the window.

Wearing what was obviously a new coat and hat, Clive sat alone in a curricle driven by the innkeeper's lad.

She turned away. Clive's business must be prospering. Perhaps he had come to gloat, or offer her another chance to invest. She wouldn't, of course, even if he arrived in the Prince Regent's barouche drawn by the finest matched pair in England. How she wished she could make him understand that!

Yet whatever his reason, if he came without Fanny, she wished Nancy and Jocelyn were there. Unfortunately, Nancy was at the village visiting some friends, and Jocelyn was at school.

Hoping that Nancy would return sooner rather than later, she removed her apron, rolled down her sleeves and shoved the errant lock of hair back into place again. She glanced at her red, wrinkled and damp hands, then wiped them on the apron before she answered the door when she heard Clive's familiar rap.

"Clive, you've come back," she said with very little enthusiasm.

He smiled, exposing his crooked yellow teeth. Then he ran an incredibly insolent gaze over her, a horrible lascivious gleam in his eyes.

A shiver of dread ran down Verity's spine as she looked past him to see the curricle going down the drive. She struggled against a nearly overwhelming impulse to call the boy back—but to do so would tell Clive he could intimidate her, and that she did not want.

"Good morning, sister. May I come in?"

Verity didn't immediately vacate the doorway. "Where is Fanny? Not ill, I hope?"

"No, she's at home."

Verity caught the scent of wine and surreptitiously wrinkled her nose. He wasn't drunk, though. Far from it. He seemed more energetic than ever before.

"Have you no baggage?" she replied as she turned slightly.

It was not much of an invitation to enter, but that didn't seem to trouble Clive in the least as he strolled past her.

"No, I don't intend to stay long."

"Oh." Relief flooded through her, only to be replaced by annoyance as Clive sauntered into the parlor with his usual proprietary air. Near the hearth, he turned toward her, and again she saw that chilling, lustful look in his eyes.

"Why have you come, Clive?"

"Why, to visit." He smiled, only this time, his smile was different, too.

She had always hated him and dreaded his visits, but never before had she felt so frightened of him, or what he might do. "For how long?"

"Whatever is the matter, dear sister?"

She straightened her shoulders. "I think you should leave, Clive."

His eyes narrowed with suspicion as he crossed his short arms. "Why, what makes you so cross today?"

She didn't answer.

"Come, sister, sit down."

"I would prefer you to leave, Clive," Verity replied through clenched teeth.

He didn't move, except to smile more, and another shiver of dread trembled along her backbone. "And I think you should be nice to me, or you will be sorry."

He started to come closer, slithering almost, like a snake with legs. "I know the truth, you see, my dear Verity."

"What truth?" she demanded as she backed away. Her heart pounded in her chest and the throbbing of her blood sounded in her ears.

He knew! How else to explain his change in

manner, his newfound confidence and bold arrogance?

But *how?*

"You really shouldn't have been so indiscreet as to discuss such a subject in the wood, where any passerby might hear that Jocelyn is not poor Daniel's child."

She couldn't breathe as her mind flew back to her meeting in the wood with Galen. She had heard nothing, but she had been thinking about Galen and her own troubles. Somebody could have been in the wood, watching and listening.

It would be like Clive to spy.

"Really, though, I must confess myself amazed that you were able to keep the secret so long," he murmured as he came closer still. "You know the kind of scandalous cad the duke has always been. Men like that love to brag about their conquests, even more than the conquest itself sometimes. Lucky for you he has been out of the country.

"Not that I would fault the duke for wanting to brag about having you, my dear," he continued in a horrible low and husky voice. "I will be tempted to shout about it from the rooftops when it is my turn."

At that statement, it was as if every insult she had ever borne, every subtle slight, every disgusting proposition and sly hint, had been distilled into one sentence uttered by a man she loathed.

"Get out," Verity ordered as she pointed to the door, her hand trembling not with fear or shame, but from pure, righteous anger.

How dare he look at her as he did? How dare he presume that she would ever let him touch her with his disgusting hands?

She was no longer alone in the world, and helpless.

Clive had forgotten, as she did not, that she need not stand alone against those who would hurt her, or her child, anymore.

Because now she had Galen.

"Get out of my house," she commanded imperiously.

Clive's eyes narrowed and his hands balled into fists. "Still the proud one, eh, Verity? So queenly, ordering me from here. This should have been *my* house. Everything you have should have been mine. Why else do you think I married that fool Fanny? For her looks?"

"Whatever you think *should* have been, this is my house, and you will leave it immediately."

"Where's Nancy?" he demanded. Then he smiled his damnable smug smile. "Here? I think not, or she would have already shown herself."

Verity's mouth went dry.

"So, we are alone. And your house is so charmingly out of the way. I daresay you could scream and scream and nobody would hear you."

Verity turned and lunged for the door, but he caught her about the waist and dragged her back into the room. "Oh, I don't think so, my dear. I don't think you want to leave just yet."

She struggled to break free, but he was stronger than she expected.

"I can see how distressing this must be for you, to realize I know all about you and the handsome duke. Very distressing indeed, given your family's already scandalous reputation."

"Take your hands off me!"

He pulled her back toward the sofa. "When I've finally gotten them on you, and when you must understand that you should let them stay there, given what I know, if you want me to keep your secret?"

"What about Fanny?"

"She doesn't know. Your secret is safe with me."

"I don't believe you."

"I assure you, my beauty, that it is—for the present. I know what I know, and I know you well enough to be certain you will do whatever I say to buy my continued silence."

"You are disgusting!"

"I'll tell everybody," he vowed as he tugged her around to face him, his wine-soaked breath hot on her face. "Everybody will find out that Jocelyn is a bastard, the bastard daughter of a bastard mother.''

''Have you considered what the Duke of Deighton will do if you harm us in *any* way?'' Verity demanded breathlessly. ''You heard *him* in the woods, too. She is blood of his blood. Do you think a man like that will sit idly by while his child is threatened—or his child's mother?''

''He doesn't care about anybody but himself.''

Clive had not seen Galen's face when she had asked him to leave them alone. He had not witnessed Galen's heart breaking before his very eyes. ''Touch a hair on Jocelyn's head or force yourself upon me, and he'll see you hang!''

Her words finally seemed to penetrate his understanding. Then that horrible smile returned. ''Rape? Really, my dear sister-in-law, you mistake my purpose. I shan't take you against your will. You will give yourself to me.''

''You must be mad!''

''Without scruples, perhaps, but not mad,'' he replied, his eyes darkening with lust. ''Give me what I desire and I will keep your secret,'' he muttered as he bent his head to kiss her.

She spit in his face.

He raised his hand and struck her hard. ''You ungrateful whore!'' he snarled. ''Who do you think you are? You're nothing but a harlot who found a fool to make a supposedly honest woman of you.

You should be *glad* I am willing to keep your secret, at any price!''

His grip tightened and she bit her lip not to cry out in pain.

''Why be so difficult?'' he demanded as he forced her down to the sofa. ''It's not as if you have your virtue to consider. And you'll be doing this for your precious Jocelyn. All you have to do is let me have you and I'll keep your secret. Think of Jocelyn and submit.''

She stilled. ''If I let you do this, do you give me your word that you won't tell anybody the Duke of Deighton is Jocelyn's father?''

His hold relaxed a little. ''Yes.''

''Go to hell, Clive.''

With all the force she could muster, Verity brought her knee up, striking him in the groin. Groaning and staggering back, Clive clutched himself. Verity scrambled to her feet.

''Blackstone!''

Verity gasped with surprise and whirled around to see Galen standing in the doorway. Relief, pure, unadulterated relief, flooded through her and joy swiftly followed as she ran to him and threw her arms around him.

As his embrace tightened about her protectively, he looked down at her with grave concern. ''Has he hurt you?''

She shook her head.

His gaze left her face to settle, with angry intensity, on Clive.

"Blackstone, it is lucky for you I have arrived in time, or you would be dead," Galen said grimly, and there was not a doubt he meant it. "I didn't think the thirty thousand pounds was going to be enough to stop you from preying on Verity, and I see I was quite right."

"Thirty thousand pounds!" Verity cried, pulling away to look at them both.

"That's what he requested when he came to see me in London, and I agreed, on the condition that he was also to stay away from you. To leave the country, in fact."

"Why should you not pay me that much?" Clive demanded. "That's what I would have had if Daniel hadn't married your whore."

Galen was across the room in an instant. He grabbed Blackstone and pulled him close, until they were nose to nose. "Call her that again, and by God, I *will* kill you."

"Galen, let him go," Verity commanded.

He glanced back at her, and after a long moment, did as she asked. She hurried toward them, taking Galen's hand in hers before she faced her enemy.

An enemy she would fear no longer. An enemy she would no longer give dominion over her. An enemy she could face and conquer with Galen at her side. "Clive, you had better give back the duke's money, or you will be charged with blackmail."

"You...you can't mean that!" Clive spluttered. "You know how people will talk. How they will treat your daughter."

"It will be difficult, of course. None know that better than I—but it cannot be more difficult than dealing with the likes of *you*. I was wrong not to realize that before, to hide us away in shame and fear."

Galen squeezed her hand and looked at her with love shining in his eyes. "And she *is* the daughter of a duke. Surely that will count for something."

He turned his triumphant gaze to Clive again. "I really think you ought to reconsider, Blackstone. If Verity is willing to let the truth be known, I would be delighted to tell the world of my daughter. Of course, it might be wiser of you to keep your knowledge to yourself." His smile grew. "Indeed, I find I am feeling quite magnanimous, so if you do keep that ugly mouth of yours shut, I will let you have the fifteen thousand pounds I've already given you as payment for your mills and to buy your passage from the country."

His expression altered to one of grim resolution. "On the condition that we never see or hear from you again."

Clive regarded them angrily for a moment, then

his bravado fled as he realized they were united in their determination. "I'll be well rid of you!" he snarled. "I hope you all rot in hell, and that brat, too."

He stormed out of the room and they heard the front door slam.

Galen put his arm around Verity. "That may not be the last we see of him."

"It doesn't matter. I would rather he get nothing, and certainly not your fifteen thousand pounds."

"If that is what it takes to free us from him, I will gladly part with it."

"Whether Clive leaves us alone or not, we are free now, Galen," Verity said, smiling gently. "Really free."

He drew her close. "Yes, we are, but I shall have him watched until he sails, nonetheless."

He bent down to press a soft kiss upon her mouth. "Besides," he murmured as his lips trailed across her cheek, "I have been thinking about what you said. Perhaps I should try to do more for mill workers, starting with showing how a mill can be run with both fairness and economy. If nothing else, I believe I would be a better mill owner than Clive was and definitely better to my workers. That must add to our victory."

She laughed softly. "It does."

Then they heard the sound of hoofbeats.

Galen let go of her and went to the window. "He's taken Harry."

"Oh, Galen!"

"Never mind. Let him go."

The front door banged open. "I just seen that Blackstone—!"

When Nancy spotted Galen, she came to an abrupt halt, sending her bonnet flying forward. She shoved it back regardless of the damage she did to its brim. "Sweet sufferin' savior! What the devil is *he* doing here?"

Chapter Fifteen

"Sit down, Nancy," Verity said calmly. "I have something to tell you."

"He hasn't come to make trouble, has he?" she demanded suspiciously. "About Jocelyn?"

"What about Jocelyn?"

"About her being his daughter, that's what," Nancy replied, still glaring at Galen while she moved as if to bar the door. "If you think we're going to let you come here and—"

"You knew about her?" Galen asked, while Verity felt for a chair and sat heavily.

She felt as winded as if she had run for miles. "All this time you knew about the duke and me?"

"O' course I did. Mr. Davis-Jones had no secrets from me. He told me before you was married. He wanted me to understand I was to be good to you. 'Nancy,' he says to me, 'I have forgiven her because I love her dearly, and you are to do the same.' So I did.'' She sniffed, then smiled. ''It wasn't hard. I never seen nor heard of a more devoted wife than you were to him.''

''Why didn't you say anything to me sooner?''

''Because you were so ashamed—and quite rightly, too. I would have made your life a misery if you hadn't been. Still, I didn't see any need to add to your shame. I was scared that Blackstone was going to find out. Every time he come here I was on tenterhooks, believe you me!''

Which probably explained her fits of temper when the Blackstones came to visit.

''Galen doesn't want to interfere,'' Verity explained. ''He wants to know her, as he should, since he has learned she exists.''

''I assure you, Nancy, I love my daughter and want only what is best for her.''

''He was willing to stay away from us completely because I thought that would be best,'' Verity confirmed.

''Then what's he doing here?'' Nancy demanded.

''He came back to warn me that Clive had discovered the truth. He arrived just in time. If you must be angry, be angry at Clive. He came on his own and wanted to use my secret to...to make me...''

''I can guess,'' Nancy growled, a look of both angry understanding and sympathy dawning. ''I knew that slimy lout was just biding his time.'' She shook her fist toward the lane. "I wish he was still here. I'd make him sorry!"

"I don't doubt that you would," Galen agreed. "I am more glad than I can say to know Verity has such a loyal friend. However, I sincerely hope we shall not be seeing Mr. Blackstone again. He has left, presumably for good."

"Thank God—and I hope you're right!" She eyed them both warily. "So you're telling me the duke's not going to make trouble?"

"No, he's not going to make trouble," Verity affirmed.

"I promise you, Nancy, I love them both too much to cause any trouble."

Nancy's face suddenly brightened with a broad smile. "I believe you," she declared with a brisk nod. "I can see it in them eyes of yours. Now, what about a spot of tea? I could use one, I'm sure."

"Yes, please," Verity answered.

With no further urging, Nancy headed for the kitchen, pausing on the threshold to look back at Galen. "Little Jocelyn's the spittin' image of you, you know. 'Cept for her eyes, o' course. But nobody'd believe Mrs. Davis-Jones ever had a dishonorable thought in her life, leastways them as knows her, so I think your secret will be safe awhile yet."

"I hope you're right," Galen said as Nancy marched out of the room.

"She knew, Galen," Verity said incredulously, coming to him. "She knew all the time. I never suspected for a moment, nor would I have believed she could keep such a thing to herself."

"Another surprise in a day of surprises."

As she led him back to the sofa, she said, "You're so pale. Are you ill?"

"Only exhausted. I had the devil of a time getting out the city, and Harry threw a shoe. I feared I was never going to get here, and at the same time, worried that if I did, I would be upsetting you for nothing."

"Because you paid to ensure our safety."

He nodded. "I only hope it's enough."

"If it isn't, I'm not afraid. I mean it, Galen," she said. "I am tired of being frightened. I will not have Jocelyn live in fear, either, as I have done. She also has a father who loves her, and I will not deny her that anymore, either."

He kissed her tenderly. Reverently. "Nevertheless, I had better leave before somebody notices I'm here. I suppose I can stay with Myron tonight, although the poor fellow will likely wonder if I've gone soft in the head running back and forth between Jefford and London."

She held him close, nestling her head against his

chest. "Or he may think you have reverted to your former impetuous ways."

"Perhaps. I wish so much I had been a better man when I first met you."

"If I had been stronger all those years ago—"

Galen shook his head. "You were young, and alone. If *I* had been stronger, I would have sent you away, or sought you out before you married. We both made mistakes, Verity. Let us have no more recriminations. What is past is past."

With a sigh, Verity nodded, feeling safe and secure at last.

He caressed her cheek. "If Nancy keeps our secret, it may be that no one else need ever know the truth about Jocelyn."

"Or it may be that Clive will tell everybody he meets." She cocked her head to look up at Galen. "It doesn't matter anymore, Galen, if all of society turned its back on me. It would be worst to have to live without you. I know that now."

His arms tightened about her. "Or it may be that my threats will work, and he will keep his mouth shut. Let us hope for the best."

"Whatever happens, Jocelyn will know the truth one day, as she should," Verity promised. "I confess I don't relish the idea of admitting what I did, but she has a right to know you are her father."

"Well, let us take that road when we must, and

not before, my love,'' he whispered as he lowered his head.

His lips met hers with loving urgency, and passion no longer constrained by secrets and past mistakes.

''Mama?''

Verity started and looked over her shoulder. Jocelyn gazed at them from the door, her eyes wide and her mouth agape. A schoolbook was cradled under her arm, and the mud on her boots revealed that she had taken the shortcut through the woods home.

''Next will come mad King George,'' Galen muttered wryly as they moved apart, although they still held hands. ''Good afternoon, Miss Davis-Jones.''

''You've come back.''

''I found it impossible to stay away.''

''You were kissing Mama.''

''I confess I was.''

''I was kissing the duke, too,'' Verity noted, determined that her daughter understand this was a good thing.

Jocelyn walked slowly into the room. ''Do you want to marry Mama?''

Galen looked at Verity and her heart pounded in her chest at the love shining in his eyes. ''Yes, very much.''

Jocelyn grinned broadly and threw her book

onto the sofa with glee. Then she gave a tremendous whoop.

"Jocelyn," Verity began, feeling that she ought to say *something,* or at least act like a respectable grown-up—even though, in truth, she felt like whooping herself.

"Please say yes, Mama!" Jocelyn pleaded eagerly. "He's so very nice. I like him so much, and I know you do, too. I want you to be happy, Mama. You're happy when you're with the duke."

Verity turned to him, her eyes brimming with happy tears.

"I do not want to disappoint Jocelyn in any way," he said before she could speak.

He knelt on one knee and took her hand gently in his. "Verity, will you do me the honor of becoming my wife?"

"Say yes, Mama, say yes!" Jocelyn cried. "Look, he's gone down on his knee and everything, just like a prince in a storybook!"

"How, then, could I say no?" Verity softly replied.

"My love," Galen cried, pulling her into his arms and kissing her passionately.

It took them a moment to remember they were not alone, and break the kiss. Then Galen immediately reached out to include Jocelyn in his loving embrace.

* * *

"Galen!" Eloise cried as her cousin entered the drawing room of her London home five days later. "What a delightful surprise! It is not like you to call in the afternoon."

Galen smiled, and inwardly girded his loins as he prepared to deliver news that would be even more of a surprise. "Good afternoon, Eloise."

Despite his resolution that he had to tell Eloise his good news and endure her voluble reaction, he hesitated. "George about?"

Eloise frowned as she resumed her seat on the gold brocade sofa and draped her arm over its curved mahogany back. "He's in his study. He told me he was going to be writing a letter to a man with a particularly fine foxhound, but he's really gone there to nap."

"Oh."

"Why? Do you need to speak with him?"

"No," Galen confessed. He sat on the delicate chair opposite her. "I have come to tell you both some wonderful news, but if he is sleeping, I will not disturb him."

Eloise straightened. "News? What news?"

"I am going to be married."

"Oh, my dear cousin!" she cried as she clapped her hands. "Lady Mary will be a perfect wife for you! So charming, so sweet, so accommodating!"

"My bride will not be Lady Mary."

"So accomplished, so pretty, so—!" Eloise blinked. "What did you say?"

"I said, my bride will not be Lady Mary."

"Then…then who?"

"I am going to marry Verity Davis-Jones."

Eloise gasped for breath like a fish out of water. "Ver…Verity Davis-Jones? You can't be serious!"

"I am very serious," he replied gravely. Then he smiled. "I love her, Eloise, and she assures me the feeling is mutual."

"Love…you *love* her?"

"I didn't mean to upset you. Shall I call a footman?"

"No, no!" she cried as she rapidly fanned herself with her hand. "It's just…such a surprise! I mean, *Verity!* When did you…how did you…?"

"I thought you liked Verity."

"Oh, but I *do!* She is a lovely woman—but she's…well, she's not…"

"Titled and rich?" he supplied for her.

"Yes!"

"I don't care."

Eloise frowned. "Of course you don't. You're a man and a duke. But people are going to talk, and there is her daughter—"

Eloise fell silent and her eyes widened as she stared at her dark-haired cousin.

"What about her daughter, Eloise?" Galen asked evenly.

His cousin blushed, swallowed hard—and met his gaze. "Nothing, Galen, nothing at all, except that she exists."

"Yes, she does, and she is going to be in my life from now on."

"Of course, yes, I see," Eloise replied. She smiled. "I see absolutely, and you may count on me, Galen." She rose and gave him a kiss on the cheek before resuming her seat. "I'm really very happy for the both of you."

As he slowly let out his breath, Galen realized just how anxious he had been about Eloise's reaction to his news, and if she would guess about Jocelyn. Fortunately, it seemed Eloise understood how he intended to deal with anybody who questioned Jocelyn's parentage. "Thank you, Eloise."

"I'm sure you'll both be very happy together."

"I know we will."

"Where will you live? Italy?"

Galen shook his head. "We know there will be some talk, and we think we must brave it out, cousin. We have done enough running away."

Eloise nodded her approval. "Very wise, Galen, very wise. Face society head-on. When is the wedding? Of course, I shall give you a party and—"

"Eloise?"

"Yes, Galen?"

''Perhaps not *that* head-on. Give us a little time, won't you? And we would like a small wedding, just friends and family, which means you and George, naturally.''

''This news will cause a sensation, Galen, no matter what you do.''

''We know, and neither Verity or I are looking forward to it.'' Then he gave her a knowing smile. ''But you don't mind making a sensation, do you, cousin? Think how it will be when you tell your friends how I fell in love at first sight and had to try so hard to win my bride's hand that when I believed it be hopeless, I was so full of despair, I contemplated suicide.''

Eloise stared at him. ''Suicide?''

''Perhaps my feelings were not quite so drastic, but I see no need to let that impede your story. You may tell them whatever you wish—within reason,'' he added, ''just so long as you make it very clear that I am utterly and completely in love with Verity and will not be pleased by rude remarks or sly innuendoes.''

''If the look you gave me a little while ago affects others as it did me, cousin, I think you have very little to fear in the way of rude remarks or sly innuendoes—to your face, at any rate.''

''I know there will be other remarks behind my back,'' he admitted. ''We cannot do anything about that.''

"Except do as you said you would and brave it out. I really do think that will be for the best. Otherwise, the speculation will take on a life of its own. When I think of some of the rumors flying about when you first went to Italy! Several people had you locked in a madhouse, you know."

"Really?"

"A few thought a foreign prison much more likely."

"I was in prison, Eloise, but one of my own making."

His cousin's eyes softened as she gave him a maternal smile. "And now I think you are finally out of it. Galen, I am truly happy for you. Both of you."

Suddenly she gasped and jumped to her feet. "I simply must tell George!" She hurried to the door, then paused on the threshold and gave Galen a wry smile as she glanced back over her shoulder. "That should take his mind off his dogs for a moment."

While Eloise was out of the room, an anxious footman appeared and came toward Galen. "If you please, Your Grace, there's a man here asking for you. He says his name's Franklin, Your Grace."

The man he had hired to keep an eye on Clive and ensure that he boarded the ship? What the devil was he doing here?

At nearly the same time, Verity hurried up the steps to Fanny's house in Heathrow. Before she could knock, Fanny threw open the door and fell sobbing into her sister-in-law's arms. "Oh, Verity, Verity, I'm so glad you've come! I don't know what to do! Oh, Clive!"

Verity gently embraced Fanny. "I got your letter, so naturally I came as soon as I could. Now let us go inside, Fanny, and I'll make us some tea, shall I?"

Sniffling, Fanny nodded and let Verity take her by the hand as if she were no older than Jocelyn, and lead her inside the small, dark house. She continued to weep and sniffle as Verity set about removing her cloak and making the tea in the cramped kitchen. She didn't know where Fanny's servant had gone, but wasn't about to ask her distraught sister-in-law.

When the kettle was filled and set on the stove, she sat at the table and regarded the woeful Fanny. "You have still not heard from him?"

"Not a word, not a line, since he left for London! I fear something terrible has happened to him. I...I know you don't like him, Verity, but I am so frightened."

With a sigh, Verity reached out and took Fanny's hand in hers. This was not going to be easy, but it had to be done. "Fanny, I have something to tell you."

"About Clive?" she asked warily.

"Yes, about Clive."

"Is he dead?" she whispered.

Verity shook her head and the haunted look in Fanny's eyes lessened. "Nevertheless, I have to say I don't think he'll be coming back."

"Not coming back?" Fanny repeated helplessly. "Then he did go to see you and not to London? What happened? What have you done?"

"I didn't do anything, Fanny, and I think you know that. But Clive wanted to do something, something despicable."

Fanny's face reddened, and more tears fell from her eyes.

"He was prevented by the Duke of Deighton."

She blanched. "The duke?"

"Fanny," Verity continued gently, "what do you know of Clive's dealings with the duke?"

"I don't know anything about Clive's dealings with anybody. He never talked about business to me. He did say he was going to London on business, though."

"He went to London to try to blackmail the duke."

Fanny gaped at her.

"It's true. He found out something, and he was going to use it against both the duke, and me."

Fanny's grip on Verity's hand tightened. "He found out about Jocelyn, didn't he?" she whispered. "I was afraid he might one day."

Verity's mouth fell open in astonishment. How many other people had Daniel told about Jocelyn? "You knew? How?"

"I didn't know, not for certain, but she didn't resemble Daniel in the least, not in appearance or manner. Nor did she look a great deal like you, so I only suspected. I had no proof of anything, and you were so good to Daniel and he loved you so much, and doted on Jocelyn..."

She began sobbing again, prompting Verity to rise and go to her, kneel beside her and put her arms tenderly about her. "You never said anything of your suspicions to Clive," she said softly, realizing that it must be so, or Clive would have used even a supposition against her long ago.

"No."

"For that you have my deepest gratitude, Fanny. But how did you know about the duke? I never told Daniel who I had been with."

"I didn't know it was the duke until I saw him. Then I saw the resemblance, and the way he looked at you." Her sister-in-law raised her tearful eyes. "Where is Clive? Did the duke have him arrested?" She started to stand. "I must go to him."

"No, he didn't have Clive arrested," Verity replied, even as she marveled at the depth of Fanny's devotion to both her brother, who deserved it, and her husband, who did not. She spoke reluctantly, knowing her words were going to hurt Fanny. "The duke gave Clive the money he wanted, with the provision that he leave the country."

She watched as the realization that Clive was alive and well, but had not returned, sank into Fanny's understanding. "I'm so sorry to have to tell you this, Fanny."

"He's left me?"

"It seems so."

Fanny buried her head in her arms and great, wrenching sobs of despair filled the room.

So did the whistle of the boiling water in the kettle, and Verity had never been so glad to hear that sound. She hurriedly prepared a strong pot of tea, found the dishes and other accoutrements, and poured Fanny a cup, fixing it as she liked.

"Fanny," she said gently, stroking her hair. "Fanny, please have some tea."

When Fanny raised her head, her expression was one of utter desolation. "Where shall I go? What shall I do? Without Clive, I...I have nothing!"

"That's not true, Fanny. You have your family—me, and Jocelyn."

"But we were so mean to you."

Verity shook her head. "Not you, Fanny. Besides, if you can forgive me as your brother could, I can forgive you for what is past, too."

"I tried not to forgive you," Fanny confessed after she finally took a sip of the hot tea. "If it wasn't for you, I would have had money and Clive would have loved me.''

Verity gazed at her sympathetically. ''He wasn't worthy of your love, Fanny.''

''But I loved him nonetheless. I'll never love anybody else.''

Verity thought the time had come to tell Fanny more. ''You may have another chance. The duke and I are getting a second chance. Why not you?''

''A second chance?''

''We are to be married.''

Not unexpectedly, Fanny began to cry again, the tears falling into her cup. Verity didn't know what to do or say, so she let Fanny weep.

Just as Fanny's sobs were beginning to grow quieter, somebody knocked on the front door, making them both jump.

''I'll see who it is,'' Verity offered.

She went down the narrow corridor and opened the door to find Galen on the step. He looked as taken aback as she was. ''Galen! Didn't you get my letter?''

''No.'' He came inside and closed the door. ''Why are you here? Where is Mrs. Blackstone?''

''Clive never came home after he left you. Fanny was desperate and wrote to me, begging me to come, poor woman.''

''Oh, God,'' Galen sighed, leaning back against the door and regarding Verity sorrowfully.

She noticed how pale he was. "What is it? What's happened?"

"Her husband is dead. He was in a tavern near the docks and there was an argument, then a brawl. If he had the money I gave him, it's gone."

They both heard a whimper like that of a wounded animal. Verity turned quickly, to see Fanny sink to the floor in a faint.

By the time Fanny woke, Galen had learned all that Fanny had told Verity. Together, they suggested Fanny allow Galen to make the arrangements for Clive's burial and take care of any business or legal matters. Fanny silently acquiesced, and Galen departed.

Verity remained and sat beside Fanny's bed, regarding her sister-in-law compassionately. "Please, Fanny, won't you come home with me to Jefford? You should be with your family."

Fanny managed a tremulous smile. "Thank you, Verity. I would like that very much."

Epilogue

Three months later, Galen slowly opened the door to his bedchamber. "Verity?" he whispered, wondering if his bride was already in bed or still disrobing. Myron and George had kept him far too long drinking toasts, in honor of the festive occasion.

But considering that George had abandoned his beloved dogs in honor of the Duke of Deighton's wedding and Galen had been living at Myron's until a week before the ceremony, he had not thought it polite to leave them too early, no matter how much he wanted to.

Nancy had long since taken a happy, cake-filled Jocelyn to bed, and the other ladies had retired not long after that.

"Verity, are you here?"

Perhaps she was in her own bedchamber, which connected to his via the dressing room. It had been a long day, what with the wedding that morning at St. George's, Grosvenor Square, small though it had been, then the wedding luncheon at Eloise's house, until they had come home with Jocelyn, Fanny, Rhodes and Nancy to another smaller supper.

He stepped farther inside. Only one small candle burned in his dressing room, leaving the larger room dark. Indeed, his bed was deep in shadows.

Perhaps Verity was making sure Jocelyn was asleep. He had never seen his daughter so happy or excited, but in that, she was quite like the rest of the wedding party.

"I'm here, Galen," Verity said softly from the vicinity of the bed.

His heartbeat quickened as he closed the door. "I can't see you."

"I'm in bed."

He had never heard a more exciting sentence in his life.

"Don't be long."

He was wrong. *This* was the most exciting thing he had ever heard.

Very aware that the woman he adored was watching him, he shrugged off his jacket and laid it over a chair. Then he started to undo his cravat with surprisingly fumbling fingers. "Jocelyn seems very happy."

"She is. I haven't seen her so delighted in a long time."

"Have you given any more thought to when you will tell her that I'm really her father?"

"When she is a little older. This has been quite an exciting few weeks for her. I would rather wait until things have calmed a little, and she is more mature."

"Whatever you think best. You know her better than I."

"I'm sorry for that, Galen. Truly sorry."

Finally getting the knot of his cravat untied, he raised his eyes to look at Verity, or as much of her as he could see in the shadows. "Remember, my love—no more recriminations. We are starting anew." Then, to lighten the mood, he said, "I must say I don't think this is fair. I didn't get to see you undress."

"Yes, you did. Ten years ago. Now it is my turn."

He grinned. She had him there, after all. "I hope I don't disappoint you."

"I don't think you will, although I must say I'm sorry you cut your hair."

"Rhodes insisted that a bridegroom shouldn't look unkempt."

"Rhodes should have asked the bride what she thought. Besides, you never looked unkempt."

Galen emitted a low chuckle. "It will grow."

He tugged off his cravat and tossed it onto the chair. "It's too bad Buck and War couldn't be here."

"Yes, but I was glad to meet Hunt. He looks as I imagine you must have when you were his age."

Galen strolled toward the bed as he began another struggle, this time with his shirt buttons. Really, he was as nervous as a lad, he thought wryly. Either that, or trembling with excited anticipation.

He rather suspected the latter. "Unfortunately, he's in a fair way to acting like the young fool I was, too," he replied. "I caught him in the pantry with one of the maids."

"Really?"

"Yes, really. And here I thought Nancy was going to rule my household with an iron fist."

"Give her time. In the meanwhile, don't say anything to Nancy about the maid. Let me speak to the girl first."

"Gladly. I'm sure you'll be a little more forgiving."

"I must be, mustn't I?"

"And I shall speak to Hunt before he goes back to school." He sighed softly. "I hope he'll listen to the voice of experience."

"I thought Fanny was looking much better, although she is still far from recovered."

"She's well rid of Clive."

"I know that, Galen, and I think, in time, she'll

see that, too. It's very sweet of Eloise to invite her to visit.''

"She's not going.''

He heard Verity move. "Why not?''

"It seems she prefers to stay here with us awhile yet.''

"Oh? Oh!'' Verity laughed softly. "Now that I think a moment, I can't say I'm surprised. Rhodes has been very solicitous. I think he's quite taken with her, and I get the impression that she's not completely averse to his attentions.''

"I would rather he be taken with Nancy. How will it look, the Duke of Deighton's wife's sister-in-law married to his valet?''

"You sound like Eloise and her gossiping friends.''

He laughed softly. "I do, and if Fanny and Rhodes care about each other, that is enough for me.''

"Well, if we're going to gossip,'' Verity said with a hint of amusement, "what about Myron and Lady Mary? Eloise assures me that they will be engaged soon.''

"Eloise is likely right about that. Myron was quite smitten with her from the start and once I was out of the running, well, he's a surprising good hunter, you know. I don't think she stood a chance.''

"I think you're underestimating Lady Mary.

She's in love with Myron. I'm sure of it, and it says much for her if she is. He is a very kind and good man.''

Straining to see his bride in the dark, able to see only the outline of her head and the covers up to her neck, he slowly drew off his shirt. ''Are you trying to make me jealous?''

''Is this slow disrobing a scheme to increase my desire?''

''Perhaps. Is it working?''

''I must confess it is,'' she answered in a low, sultry voice that made him even more aroused. ''You have a remarkable figure, you know, Galen,'' she continued in that incredibly enticing tone.

It was nearly enough to make a man forget what he was about. ''So do you.''

His hands went to his trousers and with rather more speed, he removed them, then tossed them onto the nearest chair.

''You will ruin your trousers.''

''Now you sound like Rhodes,'' he replied as he approached the bed.

''You haven't finished undressing.''

He blushed. ''Really, wife, my modesty.''

''Very well. I shall look away—although I must say I am surprised to discover you're modest at all.''

''This is…different.''

"Why?"

Now minus his drawers, he slipped between the sheets. "Because I don't want to disappoint you."

"You forget we have made love before."

"I assure you, madam, I have never forgotten that."

He felt her move closer and with both surprise and delight, realized she was naked. "So there are no secrets between us."

Galen laughed, then ran his hand along her naked leg to the curve of her hip. "And no clothes, either."

"Lie back, Galen."

"What?"

"Lie back a moment. I need to do something."

He felt the feather bed shift. "You're not putting on a nightdress, I hope?"

"No."

She got back in bed.

"That didn't take long," he observed.

"I just had to fetch something."

He nearly jumped out of the bed when he felt her fingers moving over his chest.

Her sticky fingers.

"What the devil—?" A familiar scent reached his nostrils. "Is that honey?"

"You seemed to find my childish prank with the molasses amusing."

The sensation of her fingers stroking his chest

and lingering on his nipples, was making it rather difficult to think—and when she put her leg over his, it was nearly impossible. "Is it molasses then?"

He was so aroused, it could have been coal oil, and he wouldn't have cared a jot.

"It's honey," she confirmed as she lowered her head. "I don't like the taste of molasses."

"I had no idea..." he moaned as she began to lick him clean.

"Don't you like it?"

His only answer was another moan. She shifted closer, and he felt her breasts brush against his arm. He reached out to caress her silky skin, beginning at her shoulder and moving slowly downward.

The sheet rubbed against his naked flesh and his passionate excitement intensified.

Then there was more honey, and her fingers were stroking him lower yet. Past his nipples....his navel...lower...

He bit his lip to keep from crying out as the tension built and increased more and more inside him.

Suddenly and abruptly, she straightened. "Oh, dear!"

He groaned with dismay. "What is it?"

"Hair."

"You got honey in your hair?"

"Not *my* hair. I just realized this is going to make a terrible mess."

"My dear, sweet and frustrating wife, I am a duke, and dukes have servants. Therefore, I forbid you to worry about that. All I want you to think about is us."

With that, he reached out and pulled her to him, pressing a hot kiss on her soft, honey-sweetened lips.

She leaned against him, passionate and eager— as passionate and eager as he. All thoughts of cleanliness apparently forgotten, she made a low whimper of need as she parted her lips. Needing no further enticement, he slipped his tongue into her warm, wet mouth.

Then, slowly, gently, still kissing her deeply, he pushed her down among the pillows and the soft feather bed. His lips left hers, trailing along the curve of her jaw and down her neck, over the throbbing pulse.

"There seems to be something even sweeter than your flesh here, my love," he murmured as he encountered a smear of honey on her breast.

Her only answer was another moan, and he knew full well exactly how she was feeling.

As she had never felt before.

That one night with Galen had been but a small taste of the passionate desire he was creating within her now.

She had been starving for so long. Here was a feast. She had sampled a moment's fleeting desire. Here was passion and love combined. She had stolen a brief embrace that had yielded shame and fear.

Now she was his wife, their love declared before family and friends for all the world to know.

No more secrets. No more lies.

She was free to love him as she yearned to do, to show him in a way beyond words that she belonged to him forever. "My love," she whispered.

"My wife. My beloved, beloved wife," he murmured as he placed his hand between her legs.

She inched closer, welcoming his caress. Her breathing quickened. That first time, he had never done this. She did not know anything could feel like the delicious tension increasing within her. "Oh, yes," she cried softly, arching to meet the pressure of his palm.

His fingers slipped inside her, into the waiting warmth. She writhed with pleasure, seeking more of his firm touch. All too soon, the tension crested and she cried out, carried away by throbbing release.

Then, in the next instant, he was between her legs, thrusting steadily into her, moving as she moved. She arched and pushed her legs against the feather bed, seeking better purchase, wanting him to drive deeper and deeper, to fill her completely. To be surrounded by her. Held. Cherished.

Panting, he moved faster and faster, his aroused excitement adding to hers. All thought fled, replaced by the burning need he inspired. He felt so good, so right, so perfect. She had dreamed of this so many times, yet never had the dream approached this reality. Never in her wildest imagination had she conjured such exquisite agony.

A growl burst from the back of his throat and at the same time, her anticipation exploded in a climax of waves, then ripples, of rhythmic delight.

His movements slowed, then stopped, and he lay against her, breathing heavily.

Only then did she realize she, too, was panting.

"Oh, Verity," he murmured, nuzzling her neck. "I love you."

"I love you, Galen," she replied, lifting her hand to stroke his sweat-damp hair. With her other arm, she held him close.

This was perfect. He was perfect.

She was content.

"I think we're going to need a bath in the morning," he muttered sleepily.

"We could share one."

Galen lifted his head and his gaze searched her face. "Are you in earnest?"

She grinned. "Absolutely."

"Good Lord, Verity! Where do you get these ideas?"

"Didn't Eloise warn you? I thought she told you I had a wicked imagination."

"Well, yes, I suppose she did, but I had no idea—"

Verity kissed him lightly on his adorable forehead. "If you don't want to…"

"I never said that." He laid his head back upon her soft breasts and smiled blissfully. "And here I thought I would not enjoy being married."

*   *   *   *   *

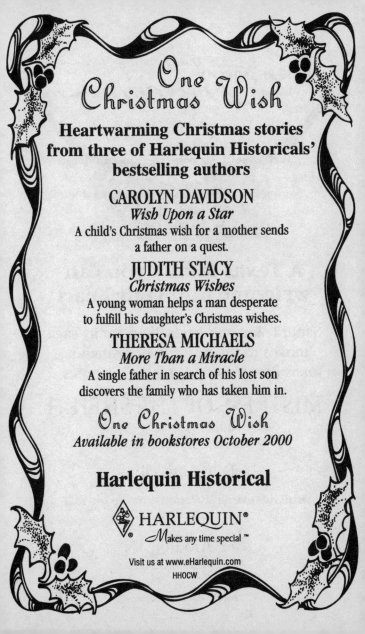

One Christmas Wish

Heartwarming Christmas stories from three of Harlequin Historicals' bestselling authors

CAROLYN DAVIDSON
Wish Upon a Star

A child's Christmas wish for a mother sends
a father on a quest.

JUDITH STACY
Christmas Wishes

A young woman helps a man desperate
to fulfill his daughter's Christmas wishes.

THERESA MICHAELS
More Than a Miracle

A single father in search of his lost son
discovers the family who has taken him in.

One Christmas Wish
Available in bookstores October 2000

Harlequin Historical

HARLEQUIN®
®
Makes any time special ™

Romance is just one click away!

online book **serials**

- ➢ *Exclusive* to our web site, get caught up in both the daily and weekly online installments of new romance stories.
- ➢ Try the Writing Round Robin. Contribute a chapter to a story created by our members. Plus, winners will get prizes.

romantic **travel**

- ➢ Want to know where the best place to kiss in New York City is, or which restaurant in Los Angeles is the most romantic? Check out our Romantic Hot Spots for the scoop.
- ➢ Share your travel tips and stories with us on the romantic travel message boards.

romantic reading **library**

- ➢ Relax as you read our collection of Romantic Poetry.
- ➢ Take a peek at the Top 10 Most Romantic Lines!

Visit us online at

www.eHarlequin.com

on Women.com Networks

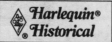

***Don't miss
an exciting opportunity
to save on the purchase of
Harlequin and Silhouette books!***

Buy any two Harlequin or
Silhouette books and save
$10.00 off future Harlequin
and Silhouette purchases

OR

buy any three
Harlequin or Silhouette books
and save **$20.00 off** future
Harlequin and Silhouette purchases.

***Watch for details
coming in October 2000!***

PHQ400

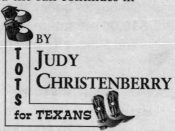

HARLEQUIN
Duets™

*Pick up a Harlequin Duets™
from August–October 2000
and receive $1.00 off the
original cover price. ***

*Experience the "lighter side of love"
in a Harlequin Duets™.
This unbeatable value just became
irresistible with our special introductory
price of $4.99 U.S./$5.99 CAN. for
2 Brand-New, Full-Length
Romantic Comedies.*

Offer available for a limited time only.
Offer applicable only to Harlequin Duets™.
*Original cover price is $5.99 U.S./$6.99 CAN.

HARLEQUIN®
SUPERROMANCE®

Here's what small-town dreams are made of!

BORN IN A SMALL TOWN

is a special 3-in-1 collection featuring

New York Times bestselling author
Debbie Macomber's brand-new Midnight Sons
title, *Midnight Sons and Daughters*

Judith Bowen's latest Men of Glory title—
The Glory Girl

Janice Kay Johnson's story, returning to
Elk Springs, Oregon—*Promise Me Picket Fences*

Join the search for romance in three small towns
in September 2000.

Available at your favorite retail outlet.

HARLEQUIN®
Makes any time special ™